John Robert Robinson, Hunter H. Robinson

The Life of Robert Coates, Better Known as 'Romeo' and 'Diamond'

Coates,

the celebrated 'Amateur of fashion'

John Robert Robinson, Hunter H. Robinson

The Life of Robert Coates, Better Known as 'Romeo' and 'Diamond' Coates,
the celebrated 'Amateur of fashion'

ISBN/EAN: 9783337219321

Printed in Europe, USA, Canada, Australia, Japan

Cover: Foto ©Raphael Reischuk / pixelio.de

More available books at **www.hansebooks.com**

ROBERT COATES.

(*Frontispiece.*)

THE

LIFE OF ROBERT COATES

BETTER KNOWN AS

'ROMEO' AND 'DIAMOND' COATES

THE CELEBRATED 'AMATEUR OF FASHION'

BY

JOHN R. AND HUNTER H. ROBINSON

CREST OF ROBERT COATES

LONDON

SAMPSON LOW, MARSTON & COMPANY

Limited

St. Dunstan's House

FETTER LANE, FLEET STREET, E.C.

1891

LONDON:
PRINTED BY GILBERT AND RIVINGTON, LD.,
ST. JOHN'S HOUSE, CLERKENWELL, E.C.

PREFACE.

APOLOGIES are so frequently used in Prefaces to biographies that in this case we do not propose to offer any, believing that a plain and impartial narrative of the career of the late Robert Coates may give entertainment to some and instruction to many. No man endured the ordeal of severe public criticism more stoically; the frequent misrepresentation of his purposes would have been resented to the utmost by many; in only one instance did he fail to ignore it.

No complete history of the English stage can be compiled without including some notice of the dramatic representations of Robert Coates. In one or two biographical and other works, some reference is made to this once famous amateur actor : these records give but scanty details, and are in error in one particular—the place of his marriage.

The portrait of Robert Coates in this volume is taken from an engraving by T. Blood, after a miniature by Newton : and that of Mrs. Coates from a plate by W. T. Fry, after a painting by F. Meyer. Both are considered faithful representations.

The authors of the present Memoir have compiled the work both from public and private sources, with exhaustive research, and, as they believe, with fulness and accuracy.

LONDON, *Aug.* 1891.

CONTENTS.

CHAPTER VII.

CHAPTER VIII.

CHAPTER IX.

CHAPTER X.

THE LIFE

OF

ROBERT COATES.

~~~~~~~~

CHAPTER I.

Antigua, its geographical features—Birth of Robert
Coates—His father's position and character for
benevolence and just dealing—Robert Coates
taken to England by his father to be educated—
His return and tour in North America—Lord
Nelson at Antigua, 1805—Robert Coates' first
appearance on the stage—Death of Alexander
Coates, 1807.

THE island of Antigua, one of the West
Indian Archipelago, is situated in lat.
17° 6′ N. and long. 61° 45′ W., and has a
circumference of about 50 miles, and an
area of 108 square miles. The island was
discovered during his second voyage in
1493 by the great navigator Christopher
Columbus, who found it peopled by only

a few Caribs, and named it after a church in Seville called Santa Maria la Antigua.

The island differs from its neighbours by being of a less mountainous nature ; its highest eminence is some 1200 feet. The first appearance of Antigua to the voyager from the sea is very uninviting; for instead of undulations covered with beautiful foliage and rich vegetation, a rough and almost barren coast presents itself. But farther inland the landscape changes to charming dales and hills, covered, when the seasons are propitious, with fields of sugar-cane, the graceful tropical bamboo, green crags with plants peculiar to intertropical regions, and flowers of every form and hue. Unfortunately the island has neither river nor springs, except the few small intermittent springs found amongst its so-called mountains.

The rainy season is somewhat uncertain, it generally extends from June to December; but the dew which in many lands makes some compensation for the absence of moisture hardly exists in Antigua. It is perhaps to this that the very equable temperature the island enjoys may be attributed, as the variation rarely exceeds 4 or 5 degrees in the twenty-four hours. The crop principally raised—and in which many of its merchants found in the earlier time a sure road to opulence— is sugar, and although coffee and cocoa have been grown, it is still upon sugar that the planter depends. The golden prime of Antigua is, it would seem, over. The shrinkage in the exports from the island is very considerable : the amount for the year 1882 was 270,846*l*. and that of 1886 only 159,971*l*., a difference of 111,160*l*. The island in propitious seasons grows some good vegetable crops, frequently sufficient for its inhabitants, who would do well to turn their attention to the raising of crops other than sugar for a staple commodity. Antigua, though of uninviting aspect to the mariner, contains two good harbours; that of St. John's, the capital, has a fair depth of water and security from winds in all quarters; the other, on the south coast of the island, called English Harbour, is one of the deepest and best to be found in the West Indian Islands, being remarkably well sheltered, and able to receive vessels of any draught. A naval hospital and dock-yard for the repairs and cleaning of ships, are situated at English Harbour.

Robert Coates, son of Alexander Coates and Dorothy his wife, was born at Antigua during the year 1772. He was their seventh child, and ultimately the only survivor of nine children, all of whom died in childhood. His father, born in 1734, was by birth a North American; this meant in those days an inhabitant of one of the English settlements in the northern part of the American continent, where his family had settled some years previously. The exact date of Alexander Coates' taking leave of the parental roof and starting in business in Antigua is difficult to fix. However, we find him in the year of the birth of his son Robert already well established there, and holding a position of high standing for integrity and wealth as a merchant, united with so benevolent a disposition and feelings so patriotic, as

to gain the love of his own people, and
also to win the admiration of the inhabitants. Mr. Coates, being a man of culti-
vated and enlightened views, naturally
desired that his son should receive a
liberal and classical education. With this
purpose in view, during the year 1780, he
embarked with Robert for London when
he was only eight years old. Here the
boy remained for many years under the
best tuition that a well-lined purse could
procure, and formed during that period
acquaintance with many persons who in
after years introduced him to the fashionable world. His education being completed, Robert returned, by his father's
desire, to Antigua. He could not but
regret the change, finding his parental
roof, albeit accompanied by the affection
of his father and mother, but a poor substitute for the sights and pleasures of the
first city in the world, and keenly feeling
the absence of those youthful friendships
which, with some natures, have a life-long
duration. The father's anxiety now was
that his son should fix upon some calling,

professional or otherwise, best adapted
to his views and inclinations. To these
proposals Robert soon replied by imparting
to his father his desire to obtain a com-
mission in the regiment of Guards of
which H.R.H. the Duke of York was
colonel. A man of his father's tempera-
ment could hardly be expected to accede
to this proposal: in fact, he vetoed it
peremptorily, and suggested that probably
his ideas respecting a future career were
not fixed, that he had better travel for a
time with the object of finding some more
suitable pursuit than that which he had
proposed. In this Robert acquiesced, and
then proceeded to make preparations for
his tour. Owing to the wars then raging
upon the Continent of Europe he was prevented from travelling alone on the beaten
path, and he ultimately decided upon
visiting his father's native land and the
adjacent States. He returned much bene-
fited in health and enlightened in mind,
the natural result of such a tour.

About this period, 1805, Antigua was
visited by the gallant Nelson with his Fleet

of ten ships in pursuit of the enemy. The advent of so illustrious a person was, of course, hailed by the Antiguans, who made all possible preparation to render him homage and bid him welcome to their isle.

A deputation of the principal inhabitants, which included Alexander Coates and his son Robert, waited upon Lord Nelson. The Admiral thanked them for their good wishes and consideration, remarking that as it was his duty to find the enemy and that he should make all sail so soon as his ships were watered, it would be impossible for him to accept their hospitality. Nelson concluded by saying that he had not been out of his ship for two years, that he could not leave it then, but must hasten to Europe, whither he feared the enemy had returned. The deputation retired much pleased with their reception, but greatly disappointed that they were not to have the honour of entertaining the brave Nelson, whom, together with the officers of his Fleet, they furnished with every luxury the island afforded during their stay. Robert Coates was much impressed

by Nelson's demeanour towards the deputation, and frequently mentioned this incident in after life.

Lord Nelson was no stranger to these
islands, having been deputed to the
command of the *Boreas* (twenty-eight guns)
in 1784, to protect British commerce from
a misunderstanding with the Americans,
who had now declared their independ-
ence, and had claimed their right to trade
with the West Indies. As the English
Government disputed this claim, Nelson
seized at Nevis four American vessels
sailing under the colours of the island,
thereby arousing great resentment on the
part of the inhabitants, who had placed
cargoes in them. The Admiralty Court
ultimately condemned the vessels and their
cargo, and Nelson was sued a year or so
later for their value, assessed at 20,000*l*.
Upon this he determined to resign his
command and quit the country, should the
Government not come forward on his
behalf. This, however, they did. During
his stay on this station he acted, in con-
unction with Captain Holloway of the

Solebar, as the chief attendant of Prince
Frederick William (afterwards William
1V.), who was voyaging among the islands
of the West Indian Archipelago. Prince
William visited Antigua, and made a
favourable impression on the inhabitants.
It was just after the Prince's visit to that
island (March 12th, 1787) that Nelson
married Mrs. Nisbet, widow of a doctor in
Nevis, who was then in her twenty-fifth
year; it was said to have been a marriage of affection upon Nelson's part, but
his later relations with Lady Hamilton
scarcely bear this out.

It was about this time that Robert
Coates first took part in amateur theatricals. These performances originated in
the dearth of public places of entertainment in Antigua, as well as the other
West Indian Islands at that period. There
were no parks or walks, no concert or ball
rooms. At one time there was some
attempt at a subscription Assembly, which
was held at a tavern kept by one named
Smith. In 1788 the first Antiguan theatre
was formed by some amateurs, who gene-

rally engaged the baud of the regiment then in garrison to act as orchestra, with the consent of its Colonel. The performers were frequently supplemented by a company of players making the tour of the West Indies, which in those days probably paid better than similar speculations of to-day.

The company would generally give the inhabitants a taste of their histrionic powers in *Hamlet, Romeo and Juliet, Othello, Macbeth,* etc., etc. Among such surroundings Robert Coates first assumed the " sock and buskin "; and many a time and oft did he make his bow to Antiguan audiences, who applauded his recitations and performances. These entertainments at last became a " hobby," which he rode hard both in his native island and afterwards in London ; in fact, so deep had the passion for the drama entered into his soul, that a profession or calling sank into unimportance ; for he appears never to have followed either, or even to have attempted to do so. After the dream of dramatic glory had taken firm hold of his imagination, the death of his father, on November 12th, 1807, stayed for a time his theatrical efforts; respect for the departed, together with small duties connected with the estate, preventing his appearance on any stage. In recording the death of Alexander Coates, a correspondent of a London magazine (*Gentleman's Magazine*, Vol. LXXVIII.) makes the following allusion, which shows the high character he bore, and the respect in which he was held by the inhabitants of Antigua, as also the benefit he conferred on the island by his patriotism.

"Died at Antigua, Alexander Coates, Esq., a gentleman who did as much good for Antigua as anyone had done for a century. Many individuals might have had their estates out of the possession of their families, had he not stepped forward, paid the mortgages, and allowed them the privilege of sending the produce of their sugar plantations where they pleased.*

* The writer by this refers, no doubt, to the terrible years of 1770 and 1778, when the island produced no crops of any kind. These years inflicted much loss upon the inhabitants.

The illiterate mind cannot say a word against such a character, as Mr. Coates might have placed his money in the British Funds, which would have been of much greater advantage, particularly in time of war; money lent as his was worth twelve per cent. But he had the lawful interest of the country, and their consigning their crop to whom they chose was an incalculable advantage and what is unusual on such loans.

"In the year 1805, when the Legislature, sanctioned by the late Lord Lavington, Captain-General of the Leeward Islands, etc., allowed the Treasurer a vote of credit for 5000*l*., Mr. Coates was applied to, but he did not at that moment think proper to lend the money, so that it might not be insinuated that he lent, not by the way of doing good to the Government, but through fear of the combined fleets of France and Spain, which were at that time threatening the island with destruction, and were making preparations at Martinique to attack Antigua. The combined fleets and armies sailed for Antigua on June 7th, 1805,

but his Majesty's troops, and the officers
and seamen of the Royal Navy, who were
at that time on the island, united by the
unanimous wish of the inhabitants, turned
out at two in the morning to oppose the
enemy's landing. They however proceeded
northwards on the 12th of the same month.
The late Admiral Viscount Nelson appeared
off Antigua with his gallant ten sail of the
line, in pursuit of the twenty-two sail of
the line of French and Spanish ships, besides frigates, etc.

" During the stay in the West Indies of
so great a naval force of the enemy and
troops to the number of 13,000, the
Government of Antigua was under the
necessity of incurring considerable expense
by a military encampment of all ranks of
the inhabitants, which lasted forty days.

" When the enemy made their appearance, their timidity was such that they
passed by without an attempt to invade.

" The encampment broke up ; Mr. Coates
then came forward, nor was it the first time
he had assisted the Government. Under
the sanction of the late Lord Lavington

and the Legislature, he now lent 10,000*l.*, which was double the sum first requested, and at a time when all danger had passed away. These facts are inscribed on the public records of Antigua. His Majesty never had a more loyal subject than Mr. Coates, and in this particular he set a most laudable example to his family. Until he was infirm with the gout he was a tall, portly and elegant person, his face was most manly and commanding. He was born April 16th, 1734, and the Almighty whom he alone feared, was pleased to take him from this life, after having sustained an untarnished reputation for seventy-three years. The great wealth of which he died possessed, except a few legacies which were immediately paid, he nobly and equally bequeathed to his family. His funeral was numerously and respectably attended."

From the foregoing, and remembering that good traits as well as idiosyncrasies are frequently hereditary, it is easy to account at this day for many of the actions of the subject of this memoir.

Robert Coates' passion for the drama was an acquired one, into which he was led originally by the abundance of time on his hands. He employed his talent in assisting others of a kindred nature to amuse the inhabitants of his native place.

The death of his father left him in possession of ample means to travel and reside where he pleased ; he was not long in arriving at a decision. Amongst all the beautiful scenery of a tropical island, and in a position to procure every luxury which it afforded, his heart leant towards London, with its balls and concerts, together with its unrivalled theatrical entertainments, not forgetting the seasons at Bath, Cheltenham and Brighton, frequented by the élite. As for the affairs occasioned by his father's decease he had little or no care. His father, doubtless struck by the way he amused himself, and fearful that he should too early get into the hands of needy and unscrupulous persons connected with the theatrical world, had devolved a certain portion of his estate upon trust, the income to be paid to his son for life, without power of anticipation ; the remainder he left to other uses ; the greater portion of this ultimately came to Robert Coates.

Being thus early relieved of personal responsibility, he determined to quit Antigua and to take up his residence in England, the place of his earliest friendships and brightest recollections.

CHAPTER II.

Robert Coates' arrival in England—Visit to Bath—
Stay at York House—Mr. Pryse Gordon—Intro-
duction to Mr. Dimond, the manager of the
Theatre Royal, Bath—First appearance before an
English audience—Performance at Brighton,
1810—Starts his curricle—Plays "Romeo" to a
Cheltenham audience, 1811.

SHORTLY after Robert Coates arrived in
London, he journeyed to the then fashionable watering-place of Bath. There he
stayed at the York House, and met Pryse
Gordon, who takes credit for having been
the first person to introduce the afterwards so well-known "Romeo" to a
British audience. It is equally certain
that had not this opportunity occurred,
other means would soon have been found
to secure the long-sought gratification.
Mr. Pryse Gordon's account of his first
meeting with Mr. Coates, and his ultimate
introduction to Mr. Dimond, the then
manager of the Theatre Royal, Bath, by

C

him, is so racily given in his Memoirs, published some sixty years since, that we transcribe it :—" I consider myself as having been the means of first bringing out the celebrated ' Romeo ' Coates on the British stage, one of the most singular circumstances in my life. In the year 1809 I was at Bath and stayed at the York House, where I found this gentleman an inmate, and we generally met in the coffee-room at breakfast. He shortly attracted my notice by rehearsing passages from Shakespeare during his morning meal, with a tone and gesture extremely striking both to the eye and the ear ; and, though we were strangers to each other, I could not help complimenting him on the beauty of his recitations, although he did *not always stick to his author's text*. On one occasion I took the liberty of correcting a passage from *Romeo and Juliet*. ' Aye,' said he, ' that is the reading I know, for I have the play by heart, but I think I have improved upon it.' I bowed with submission, acknowledging I was not a profound critic.   This led to a dissertation on the merits of this fine tragedy. When he informed me that he had frequently performed the part of ' Romeo ' at Antigua, of which island he was a native—adding that he always travelled with the dress of that character amongst his other garments—I lamented that, with the extraordinary talents he seemed to .possess, he had not gratified the English public with a specimen of his powers, or joined the amateurs of private theatricals, and mentioned a Mr. Methuen, who made a great noise at the time, as a first-rate performer. ' I am ready and willing,' replied our Roscius, ' to play " Romeo " to a Bath audience, if the manager will get up the play and give me a good " Juliet ; " my costume is superb and adorned with diamonds, but I have not the advantage of knowing the manager, Dimonds.' After laughing at this excellent pun, in which he heartily joined, I observed that I was acquainted with this gentleman, and would either make the necessary arrangements or give him a line of introduction, as he preferred. He chose the latter; and so eager was he to gratify the Bath public during the height of the season, that as soon as he had discussed a brace of muffins and so many eggs, he set off to interview the manager with his credentials.

"In an hour he returned, full of wrath and indignation at the cavalier reception he had met with. 'The fellow,' said he, 'has treated me in a manner I am not accustomed to, and I have a great mind to call him to account for his impertinence and rude behaviour. I will show him I can play *Carte and Tierce;*' and, putting himself in an offensive attitude, he thrust at a baize door with his cane, to the astonishment of the waiters and the terror of an old gentleman sitting in the corner with a newspaper. I had some difficulty in appeasing his anger. 'This is,' I said, 'Diamond cut *Dimond*,' ('Oh, very good, ha, ha!' he replied, interrupting me), 'but I will call on the manager, and he shall make you a proper *Amende*, and when he finds you a man of *fashion* and *fortune* instead of an *adventurer*, which perhaps he might have supposed from not having the honour of knowing you, I am sure he will be but too happy to receive you on his boards.'

"This satisfied Mr. Coates, and I promised to make the necessary arrangements without delay. My friend, Mr. Scrope Davies, was at this time in Bath ; I communicated the affair to him, into which he warmly entered, recommending, as a preliminary step, to consult Lady Belmore and some other ladies of *haut ton*, whose curiosity we readily excited, and in the course of the morning a large party agreed to fill the lower boxes. With this assurance I found no further difficulty on the part of the manager, and the play was fixed for the following week (February 9th, 1809). Mr. Dimond having made his peace with the debutant, and advertised 'That a gentleman of fashion would make his appearance for the first time in England,' every box was speedily secured. In order that Mr. Coates might have a favourable reception (which, however, could not be doubted), I contrived, with the assistance of my friends, to plant in the centre of the pit a score of abigails and butlers, who, with a large party in the lower boxes, received 'Romeo' on his appearance on the stage with three distinct peals of applause. Never was a greater *furore* heard in the Bath Theatre even in the best days of Mrs. Siddons.

" The first act went off quietly, but as the play proceeded there were some symptoms of displeasure from the *gallery*, which were hissed down by the better-bred part of the audience. In the balcony-scene, some rascals, envious no doubt of the *Amateur* actor, hissed in their turn and threw apples and orange-peel on the stage; others encored certain passages, laughed when they ought to have cried, and some individuals from a side box were extremely rude in calling, ' Off! off ! ' ' Romeo,' who had hitherto conducted himself with great equanimity, could no longer submit to such ungenerous behaviour. He turned to the box from whence the sounds proceeded, and, crossing his arms, looked at the offending party with great scorn and contempt, when the curtain dropped amidst thundering applause! In act the 5th, when the hero seizes a crowbar to break into Juliet's tomb, the clamour was so great that the drop fell to rise no more. Thus, from bad taste, spleen and envy, was one of the finest actors that had appeared upon the English stage since the days of *Master Betty* damned by the audience of a provincial town—to its eternal disgrace. Fortunately, Mr. Coates had excellent nerves, and treated his critics with the contempt they merited, receiving the congratulations of the most respectable part of the spectators with a modest assurance. A few nights after this unexpected defeat there was a Subscription-ball at the York House, of which I had the honour of being one of the managers, under the direction of four lady patronesses, who instructed me to invite Mr. Coates to this *fête* in token of their high appreciation of his merits. He accepted the invitation; and on my suggestion, appeared in the costume of 'Romeo.' After supper he was prevailed upon to recite 'Bucks have at ye all'

(which we shall have cause to mention once
or twice again, so leave the fuller descrip-
tion of this monologue for another chapter),
and, mounted on the table among the
glasses and decanters, as well as sweet-
meats and other knick-knacks, he recited
this in the most admirable manner ; and, I
need hardly add, gained the greatest
applause."

In the play just mentioned Miss Jameson
appeared as " Juliet," and Mrs. Groves took
that of the nurse ; both appear to have
been good representatives of the characters.
The results of the night's performance may
be attributed to want of breadth in the
audience, who in those times were very
exacting, and received any departure from
the text, or any change made in the
representing of a well-known character,
with marked disapprobation. In the days
of which we are writing, the amusements,
notably the indoor ones, were most circum-
scribed, so that it is small wonder that
the visitants of the theatres were exceedingly jealous of innovations creeping
in, which might detract from the tone of

their single place of indoor entertainment. It is well for many lessees and managers that the play-loving public of the present day are not so difficult to please, for now a person, scarce middle age, can find Shakespearian representations produced, and many of the characters rendered far differently to when Kean, Kemble, and other delineators of Shakespeare's plays were acting, and whom they may have seen. In many instances, to give a play and character a new dress and rendering is now to become famous, and frequently leads to highest eminence in the theatrical profession. Unfortunately for Mr. Coates he was not in touch with his audience in the above matters; what cared they if he appeared as " Romeo " (and probably following the taste for bright and striking colours which all inhabitants in tropical climes possess in a more or less marked degree) in a spangled cloak of sky-blue silk, crimson pantaloons and a white hat trimmed with feathers, or that the ornament upon the hat glistened with diamonds—which likewise appeared on his knee and shoe buckles—or for any new giving of the text ? These were all as nothing to them. They came to see the " Romeo " they had always seen and as acted by the great artists of the day, but not finding their idea of Shakespearian drama adhered to they rebelled ; likewise also forgetting that the actor who had performed for their amusement and his own pleasure was only an amateur, and therefore entitled to more latitude than a professed disciple of Thespis would be. This did not form any excuse in their judgment, whilst the majority received the player with as much criticism as they would a new piece or a second-rate professional seeking their suffrages in a first-class character, and which at first blush they had determined to condemn. This did not deter Mr. Coates from proceeding in his hobby, upon every opportunity that presented itself, and he trusted in time, and by favour, to win his way to the heart of the play-going public.

Mr. Coates' next attempt was at Brighton, then just beginning to emerge from obscurity as a fishing village. This

performance was of so small a nature,—
evidently undertaken for the gratification
of a few personal friends—that but little
record was made of it.

The writer of the theatrical critiques
in the *News* of September 8th, 1811,
endeavours to raise a laugh at Mr. Coates,
by stating that "his performance at
Brighton last year astonished the aquatics
and submarines of the Sussex coast." He
was now fairly launched upon the stage,
and amongst those who frequented the
circles of fashionable life, more frequently
met with then than now at English
watering-places and seaside resorts.

As a rich bachelor, somewhat anxious
for notoriety, as well as fond of display
and dress, Mr. Coates about this period
introduced to the gaze of the astonished
Londoners his well-known curricle, which
earned for him another sobriquet, that of
" curricle " Coates. Whence the original
idea emanated of this extraordinary
vehicle it is difficult to say. Its style
was so unique that Mr. Coates has been
always looked upon as its originator. We

think that he must have taken the idea
from the celebrated Beau Fielding, a
fashionable star of a century before, and
of whom the *Tatler* tells that he rode
in a Tumbril of less than ordinary size, to
show off the fine proportion of his limbs
and the grandeur of his person to the best
advantage. Others compared the vehicle
the beau rode in to a sea-shell, accompany-
ing which were a dozen tall fellows dressed
in black and yellow. The last feature
Mr. Coates did not imitate ; but his
curricle is described by those who frequently saw it as one of the neatest
vehicles ever turned out of Long Acre.
Its shape was that of a scallop shell ;
the outside was painted a beautiful rich
lake colour, and bore its owner's heraldic
device—a cock, life-size, with outspread
wings, and over this the motto, "While
I live I'll crow." The step to enter the
vehicle was also in the form of a cock.
The interior was richly lined and uphol-
stered, and the whole mounted upon light
springs with a pair of high wheels picked
out in well-chosen colours. The vehicle

was drawn by two white horses of faultless figure and action, and which must
have been matched and acquired at great
cost. Their trappings were of the latest
fashion and ornamented with the crowing
cock in silver. The horses were driven
in pair, and the splinter bar was surmounted by a carved brass rod; on top
of this stood a plated cock, crowing. An
equipage such as this, driven by a person
dressed in the height of fashion, could
not fail to attract public attention,
whether in The Row, Pall Mall, or Bond
Street; it was admired as much for its
unique appearance as for the well-
groomed and trained horses attached to
it. The effect desired, no doubt, was
highly gratifying to its owner, who by
this means became well known to the
London populace long before he presented
himself before them on the stage. Mr.
Coates did not confine his drives to
the immediate vicinities of St. James's
and St. George's, but frequently drove
into the city, where the curricle was often
seen standing outside the Bank of Eng-

land, whilst its owner was transacting business within. By this means he became more widely known than ever.

Having so far raised the curiosity of those he wished to propitiate, he now took his leave of London for a time, and went with other persons of rank and fashion to Cheltenham, where, for the gratification of a few friends, he impersonated the character of "Romeo." This performance being of a somewhat private nature, no public record of importance respecting it exists, though the *News* of September 15th, 1811, made an anecdote as the outcome of this performance. We have before remarked that Mr. Coates generally wore about his person a profusion of valuable diamonds, part of a collection he inherited from his father. Some of these he wore on this night. At the end of Scene V., Act II., he repeated the lines, "Oh! let us hence. I stand on sudden haste"; but, instead of quitting the stage, he glanced about for a diamond knee-buckle, which he had noticed as missing before the conclusion of his sentence.

The prompter, not knowing the object of his search, said, " Come off, come off ! "   To this Mr. Coates replied, that "he would so soon as he found his buckle,"—no great cause for mirth to the loser, had he not almost immediately after found his treasure, and made the exit demanded by the play.   The humorous side of this episode, to the audience, was the stopping on the stage after the conclusion of the lines announcing his hasty departure ; this might have passed off unnoticed had they known the cause of Mr. Coates' staying.   The efforts of the amateur actor, however, appear to have been well received, inasmuch as he determined to make his début to a London audience at the very earliest opportunity.

CHAPTER III.

Mr. Coates' appearance at the Richmond Theatre, September 4th, 1811—Miss Tylney Long and Mr. Coates—The satirical coloured plate respecting them in *Scourge*—Mr. Coates' first appearance on the London stage at the Haymarket, December 9th, 1811—His reception—Letter to the *Morning Herald*, December 11th, 1811—Notes thereon.

MR. COATES appeared at the Theatre Royal, Richmond, on the 4th of September, 1811, in response to a call from several of his friends in that neighbourhood, who, knowing his proclivities for dramatic impersonations, asked him " to oblige " by taking his old character of " Romeo." To this request he acceded, and the boxes were one and all taken before the performance was regularly announced in the play-bills.

On the night in question, the theatre was packed from floor to ceiling with the fashion and beauty of the charming Surrey retreat. Amongst so large an audience, there were sure to be many who came for curiosity's sake alone, as well as others for the purpose of " roasting " the amateur, an amusement much indulged in by would-be wits and bucks of the period. The representation was on the whole better received than the Bath performance, and ran its entire length, though some " slightly elevated " fashionable young men, who had most probably been dining before they arrived, endeavoured to cause annoyance by laughing when the hero poisoned himself. They were, however, promptly put down by a counter-demonstration in Mr. Coates' favour by the ladies, with whom he was a general favourite, and this turned disapprobation into applause.

Thus encouraged, Mr. Coates, at the conclusion of the play, was requested to oblige the audience by reciting " Bucks, have at ye all."* This monologue we may

---

* Several detractors of this gentleman insinuated that he wrote the lines, or had them written for him ; neither theory is correct. The production is the work

mention as being rendered by Mr. Coates
on several other occasions; we here give
it in detail,—

"BUCKS, HAVE AT YE ALL."

" YE social friends of claret and of wit,
Where'er dispersed in social groups ye sit,
Whether below ye gild the glittering scene
Or in the upper regions oft have been,
Ye Bucks, assembled at your ranger's call,
D—n me, I know you, and have at ye all.
The motive here that sets our Bucks on fire,
The generous wish, the first and last desire.
If you with plaudits echo to renown,
Or urged with fury tear the benches down,
'Tis still the same, to one God ye prate,
To show your judgment and approve your taste.
'Tis not in nature for ye to be quiet,
No, d—n me, " Bucks " exist but in a riot.
For instance now—To please the ear and charm the
     admiring crowd,
Your Bucks of the boxes sneer and talk aloud,
To the green-room next with joyous speed you run.
Hilly ho ! ho ! my Bucks ! well, d—n it, what's the
     fun ?
Though Shakespeare speaks, regardless of the play
Ye laugh and loll the sprightly hours away;
For to seem sensible of real merit,
Oh ! damme, it's low, it's vulgar, beneath us lads of
     spirit !
Your Bucks of the pit are miracles of learning,
Who point out faults to show their own discerning ;
And critic like, bestriding martyred sense,
Proclaim their genius and vast consequence.
The sidelong row, whose keener views of bliss
Are chiefly centred in some favourite miss.

---

of one Thomas Mozeen, an actor who flourished in the
middle of the last century—1757.

A set of jovial Bucks, who here resort,
Flush from the tavern reeling, ripe from port,
Wak'd from their dreams, oft join the general roar
With bravo ! bravo ! bravissimo ! and damme, encore !
Or skipping that, behold ! another row,
Supplied by citizens or smiling beau,
Addressing miss, whose cardinal protection
Keeps her quite safe from rare'rous detraction :
Whose lively eyes beneath a down-drawn hat
Give hints she loves a little chit-a-chat.
Ye Bucks above, who range like gods at large,
Nay ! pray don't grin, but listen to your charge ;
You, who design to change this scene of raillery
And out-talk players in the upper gallery.
Oh, there's a youth and one of the sprightly sort,
I don't mean you—damme, you've no features for it—
Who slyly sulks to hidden station
(While players follow their vocation),
Whistle off ! off ! off ! nosey, roast beef, there's educa-
        tion.
Now I've explored this mimic world quite through
And set each country's little faults to view,
In the right sense receive the well-meant jest,
And keep the moral still within your breast,
Convinced I'd not in heart or tongue offend,
Your hands acquit me, if I've gained my end."

To this Mr. Coates added the following, which had been written for him to use in augmenting the foregoing verses, as well as for silencing the noisy and rebellious beaux, who frequently annoyed the audience and himself during the progress of the play. The present occasion he deemed opportune, and gave the lines for the first time at this theatre.

" Ye Bucks of the boxes there (pointing), who roar
    and reel,
Too drunk to listen and too proud to feel !
Whose flinty hearts are proof against despair !
Whose vast estates are neither here nor there,
Who drive with four-in-hands as moderns must,
Smother philosophy and take the dust ;
Who brave the demon and his imp below,
Yet tremble at John Doe and Richard Roe ;
Talk slang with grooms, old granny Justice hoax,
And graduate with coachmen on the box ;
Cut out a midge's eye upon the wing ;
Who pamper prize-fighters and keep their ring,
Who scatter Fortune's precious gifts abroad,
Who quiz the virtues and give soup to fraud,
Coax a young cit to drive, who'd cut a dash,
Then call for dice, and poll him of his cash :
Such high-toned joys and elegance be thine,
To pay my tradesmen and be just, is mine.
No creditor deprived of honest bread
Mocks my swollen arrogance and shakes his head.
Chacun a son goût.   Say, is't not well ?
You shout, ' Push on ! ' I, ' *Vive la bagatelle !* ' "

This fairly turned the tables upon the
little clique in the box, who had come to
interrupt the performers and to annoy the
audience; they were much surprised at
receiving such a Roland for an Oliver, as
well as at the non-success of their plans.

Mr. Coates had met in society, during
this year, Miss Tylney Long, heiress of
Sir James Tylney Long, Bart., of Dray-
cott, Wilts, and Wanstead House, Essex ;

and he, along with many others, became
enamoured of her. To give a complete
list of this lady's suitors would be futile,
as they were of all ranks and degrees of
wealth ; notably among them was H.R.H.
the Duke of Clarence, afterwards William
IV. Whether all these were attracted
simply by the personal charms of the lady,
or whether the attraction was of a more
weighty nature—gold—we will not be so
uncharitable as to ask. Then, as now,
heiresses with nearly 60,000*l.* a year, besides
accumulations of some 300,000*l.* sterling,
do not lack admirers ; this was Miss
Tylney Long's case. Another of her
devotees was the then well-known Baron
Ferdinand de Geramb, at that period much
sought after by fashionable society, and
to whom we shall allude again. This
personage became acquainted with Mr.
Coates during his residence in London.
Both the Baron and Mr. Coates had the
deepest regard for the highly-gifted and
wealthy Miss Tylney Long. It is not assumed for a moment that this lady gave any
encouragement to these two of her suitors,

or to any one of them—prince or peer
—excepting the gentleman she eventually
married, an event which we shall chronicle
in due order.   Mr. Coates thought it best
to approach the object of his admiration
by poems and odes.   Of these some few
were sent, but they did not achieve the
desired success.   This matter formed a
subject of grievance between Mr. Coates
and another lady, of which the reader
shall be informed later on.

The above incidents are all taken notice
of by the *Scourge*, a satirical journal,
which was published for a few years
during the first two decades of the present
century.   The coloured plate particularly
alluded to is to be found in Vol. II. as a
frontispiece to the December No. for
1811, and is after an etching by George
Cruikshank, entitled, "Princely Piety, or
the Worshipper at Wanstead."   In the
centre is Miss Tylney Long, seated upon a
dais, draped in crimson and gold, and
reached by five steps, carpeted in similar
colours ; the first of these is marked
Infancy, ten ; the second, Puberty, fifteen ;

the third, Womanhood, twenty; the fourth,
Discretion, twenty-five; and the fifth, Old-
maidism, thirty. On the right is H.R.H.
the Duke of Clarence, upon whom Mrs.
Jordan is emptying a vial of her wrath,
from which various diminutive persons
are falling, some in military and naval
costumes, she remarking, " False, faithless
Clarence, behold thy children. *Hem !
Shakespeare !* " The Duke is thrusting
back Baron Ferdinand de Geramb, who is
on his knees surrounded by bags of gold,
the result of his various achievements,
secret intelligence, etc. On the left is a
fool with his cap and bells, playing a violin,
to which two personages are dancing. In
front of these, upon their knees at the foot
of the steps, are two persons; one of these
is an old beau with his eye-glass raised,
and a petition in his hand (much
resembling Sir Lumley Skeffington); the
other is Mr. Robert Coates, whose head
supports a cock crowing " Cock-a-doodle-
doo." Romeo's hat and feathers are lying
by his side, and one hand is outstretched,
the other is placed on his heart, while in

front are various papers marked " Odes," etc.

Mr. Coates was now a recognized " Lion," and with other idiosyncrasies was deeply attached to his old love, the stage. Among the host of those who fret and strut their hour on the boards were many then, as now, with whom Fortune had dealt unkindly, or whom improvident habits made a burden to their more successful and thrifty fellow-actors. Mr. Coates was very frequently asked for aid, either in the form of a loan or gift from such persons, and not unfrequently to give his services for their benefit. The mere announcement of Mr. Coates' name was a guarantee of a full house. Mr. Coates when appealed to was almost always ready to render assistance in any way demanded for a charitable purpose ; and we fear that his good nature was frequently imposed upon by those eager to act upon the credulity of others. It may be re- membered that his father was well known for his charitable and benevolent dis- position. This in a great measure his son inherited. Mr. Coates, while being most anxious to gratify his own taste for theatrical representations at every possible opportunity, now deemed it necessary that his labours should take a practical turn, and be of some benefit to his fellow-creatures, as well as an amusement to himself and friends. After this resolve, and during his theatrical career, we find him almost without exception playing on behalf of some actor, or a widow and children, or appearing on the benefit night of some well-known manager, such as Raymond. With the above laudable objects in view, what mattered it that the character personated by Mr. Coates in the play was not rendered in such a way as Garrick or Kemble would have presented it? although the houses to witness Mr. Coates' acting were nearly always as large as those commanded by either of these eminent actors in their palmiest days. The writers of the theatrical critiques about this time looked upon the amateur actor as one seeking for Thespian fame, in order to become a professional tragedian. Nothing was farther from this gentleman's thoughts or wishes ; he acted simply for his own pleasure, but such a motive was almost incomprehensible to the writers of theatrical articles of those days. No amateur of the present time, however famous, could command from one to two columns in the leading newspapers of the day, whatever his performance might be; but Mr. Coates was accorded such ample notice on more than one occasion. There is therefore small cause for wonder that with such an advertisement gratuitously given (although frequently from an adverse point of view), the theatres were crowded to repletion whenever he performed. Probably there were those who wished to judge for themselves of the merits of Mr. Coates, but many would take their cue from the daily papers, and go to laugh and condemn because they were prejudiced.

Mr. Coates' first appearance before a London audience was on the 9th December, 1811, at the Haymarket Theatre "for the benefit of the widow Fairbur," so the bills announced, but we think the name and sex were assumed ; the real person being a man well known in theatrical circles of the time. However, the question need not be discussed here, suffice it to say that Mr. Coates appeared that evening for the benefit of a charitable purpose, which, doubtless, had his sympathies, or he would not have acted ostensibly for that purpose. The character he delineated was the gay " Lothario " in Rowe's Tragedy of *The Fair Penitent*, a part he had never played before in England, and one acknowledged to be difficult for any amateur to attempt. This being his first performance before a London audience, there were naturally many who took advantage of his appearance to be present, having heard or read of his previous impersonations at Bath, Brighton, Cheltenham, and Richmond. In fact, so great was the desire on the part of the public to witness the acting of the amateur, that long before the play began the house was crowded from floor to ceiling, and it was computed that at least one thousand persons were turned away from the box entrance alone. Many, to whom money was a secondary consideration, besieged the stage door and offered as much as five pounds for a single admission to go behind the scenes. Of course they were refused, though others were there as friends of the actors, likewise some few who had obtained admission for the express purpose of annoying Mr. Coates, and who acted several times during the progress of the piece in unison with their friends who sat in various parts of the house. No such vast concourse ever gathered together to witness an amateur sustaining the principal character in a piece, only one occasion, indeed, had approached it; this was when an amateur named Sir Francis Delaval had played "Othello" in the time of Garrick. Among the persons of rank and fashion present to witness Mr. Coates' rendering of the character of "Lothario" on this evening, were the Duke of Brunswick, the Duke of Devonshire, the Portuguese

Ambassador, the Earl of Kinnoull and family, Viscount Castlereagh, Baron de Geramb, Sir Godfrey Webster, Sir Charles Coote and family, etc., etc.

Shortly after the doors opened, it was noticed by many that a strong contingent had obtained admission for the purpose of annoying the actors and preventing the progress of the piece. They began their obstruction upon the arrival of the Baron de Geramb, receiving that personage with hisses and shouts of disapprobation; but some of the audience, thinking this somewhat harsh treatment to bestow on an illustrious foreigner and a friend of the Regent, began to applaud him vigorously; and presently the malcontents themselves joined in the applause. The house had now been open an hour, and the performance had been timed to commence at 6.30; but 7 o'clock had arrived without the raising of the curtain. After some minutes' further delay, Mr. Coates made his bow to the audience at large and in the boxes, notably to the one occupied by Baron de Geramb. The noise upon the

Amateur's appearing was deafening, and consisted of all the well-known shouts of favour, mingled with catcalls, whistling and cries of " Cock-a-doodle-doo " from those who came with the avowed purpose of condemnation. The habiliments of Mr. Coates were very rich, his dress being of a species of silk so woven as to give it the appearance of chased silver ; from his shoulders hung a mantle of pink silk, edged with bullion fringe ; around his neck was a kind of gorget, richly set with jewels, and at his side was a handsome gold-hilted sword. Coates' head-dress was composed of a Spanish hat surmounted by tall white plumes, while his feet were encased in shoes of the same material as his dress, and these were fastened with large diamond buckles. The play proceeded for a time, when those bent on making an uproar prevented the actors from being heard by their discordant noises and yells. Mr. Coates had hitherto done his best to obtain a hearing by patiently waiting for a moment or two when any sudden outburst of clamour occurred; but finding this manner of progressing tedious to himself and to the genteel portion of the audience, he now stepped forward, and said,—" If it be the wish of the nobility and gentry that this play should proceed, *I* will return the money to those noisy persons to go away." This brief speech was much applauded by those who came to hear Mr. Coates, and as vigorously decried by the obstructionists, so that it was some few minutes before sufficient silence was obtained for the piece to proceed, when it again met with determined opposition from the inimical portion of those present, and had to be abandoned at the conclusion of the fourth Act. The audience, however, retained their seats, expecting that the curtain would rise for the concluding Act. In this they were disappointed, but Mr. Coates, in accordance with the desire of the management and those interested, promised to recite the monologue named " The Hobbies " so soon as he had changed his attire. This done, he

appeared before the curtain and gave
as follows :—

"THE HOBBIES."

" Dryden observes, and he was wondrous wise,
Men are but children of a larger size ;
And honest Shandy, that odd winning droll,
On hobbies through life's journeys makes us stroll,
While some on wilful, headlong tits so light,
Are often thrown, and left in woeful pl'ght.
For hobbies are ofttimes hard-mouth'd and stubborn,
And difficult almost as wives to govern.
The statesman's favourite hobby is a place,
But his hobby oft falls lame and leaves the chase.
The soldiers' hobby in the time of war
Is battles, breaches, ambuscades and scars.
In peace how different then their trade is,
For then the soldiers' hobby is the ladies.
The ladies !   Aye, the ladies now and then
Can get astride their hobbies like the men ;
Then, Lord bless us, none can stand before 'em,
Churches and five-bar gates they skip and fly o'er 'em.
And what's more strange in every age and clime
They'll ride you several hobbies at a time.
Their lovers and their husbands, too, by fits
They transform into manageable tits.
And then they jockey us with so much ease,
We amble, trot and gallop, just as they please.
Clients are lawyers' hobbies, but their curse is—
That law jockeys always gallop hard for purses !
Onward they drive and never do they stop—
Till the poor foundered clients breathless drop.
The statesman's hobby is famed for sportive tricks
And fiddlers ride upon their fiddle-sticks,
The sailors' hobby is the triumphant wave,
A head to conquer, humanity to save.
Sailors love singing, but not such notes
As squeak bad English in Italian throats.

'Give me,' says he, 'a song that I can sing,
Here's " Rule Britannia " and " God save the King." '
Our manager, too—but let me look around—
His hobby in this theatre is to be found,
A stately nag ; and to obtain your praise
He tries *his* hobby a thousand different ways.
So far, I own him right; but, *entre nous*,
He rides his hobby and his actors too.
Onward he drives and never looks behind him,
And a d---d spurring jockey we all find him.
But now, methinks, I hear you say to me,
' You, my good sir, that are so wondrous free
With others, what may your hobby be ?'
My hobby is—may it prove safe and clever—
Sound wind and limb, a grateful, fond endeavour
To gain what most I wish—your patronage and
   favour."

With this the performance—one that
all present would remember—concluded.
Apropos of the monologue just given, one
of the critics in a well-known newspaper
of that day credited Mr. Coates with its
authorship. Whether he intended this as
a joke, or whether his error arose from
want of knowledge we cannot say; the
lines appear in a volume of Epilogues,
Songs, &c., published in 1809, and before
Mr. Coates appeared on the stage in this
country. It is true that names were
interpolated here and there—" Lord
Wellington's "—but this alone did not

E

constitute authorship ; and judging from appearances, the monologue is much older than the time attributed to it : possibly it is one often selected for theatrical recitation and much appreciated in its time.

The criticisms that appeared in the daily papers upon the above performance were unusually severe, and in many respects quite uncalled for, when we take into consideration not only the purpose for which Mr. Coates' services were gratuitously given, but the zeal of the amateur actor for appearing upon the public stage as a gentleman player. Possibly the writers of these articles were led away by the noisy demonstration of a clique present for no other purpose than to annoy Mr. Coates, whatever his acting or rendering of the character, whether good or bad. At all events, many of these critics so far overstepped the bounds of their legitimate mission, as to draw forth the following letter from Mr. Coates, which appeared in the *Morning Herald* of December 12th 1811. This instance, so

far as we have been able to find, is the
only one in which he ever personally
noticed many of the obnoxious (and in
several cases unfair) articles concerning
his dramatic efforts, that appeared from
time to time in the various publications of
the day.

" *To the Editor of the* ' MORNING HERALD.'

"SIR,—Various gross misrepresentations
having appeared relative to my late performance of 'Lothario' at the Haymarket Theatre, I beg leave to offer a
refutation of them through the medium of
your valuable and fashionable paper.

"It has been asserted that when I
addressed the audience I said 'that because I acted from a motive of benevolence, I ought to be applauded'; but
the truth is, I merely said, 'Ladies and
gentlemen, it is a very unusual thing for
a gentleman placed in my position in life
to appear before you on a public stage,
but allow me to observe that all persons
who pay their money have a right to enter
a theatre, but when they come into that

theatre with an avowed determination to disturb the public peace, every well-disposed auditor ought to set his face against such base conduct. If it is the wish of the nobility and gentry that the play should be concluded, and those noisy people will leave the theatre, and have their money returned, I will undertake to make up the deficiency to the widow; and permit me likewise to say that I hope soon to gratify my feelings by playing at the King's Theatre for the relief of the widows and orphans of our brave countrymen and our allies, who have so nobly shed their blood in the common cause.'

"That there was a conspiracy formed previous to the night's representation, for the shameful purpose of creating tumult in the theatre, at all events, can scarcely be doubted by any who were present at that outrage. It appeared there were about thirty or forty fellows placed in the pit and galleries determined to keep up one continued row, and annoy the sober and dignified part of the audience by clamour and insolence, for the acting of

Miss Sydney or Mr. Scriven was not more applauded than my own feeble endeavours to please, though neither of them would disgrace their profession at either of the theatres ; that comparative species of delicacy which is shown towards females, even by savages, was wholly disdained and disregarded by these rioters. Everything upon the stage on that occasion was to be particularly reprobated, although the efforts to entertain (even were they ineffectual) were exerted in a cause of benevolence to which none need have subscribed who were adverse to such virtuous purposes.

" It is evident from the trial of ' Macklin v. Leigh and Others,' that the law of the land does not authorize such wanton measures. The situation of an actor would be truly miserable if it were in the power of a band of tipsy wretches to issue from a tavern or *cabaret*, and drive a good man from his lawful occupation whenever their hatred or caprice might urge them to be whimsical or unjust.

" In regard to the innumerable attacks

that have been made upon my lineaments and person in the public prints, I have only to observe, that as I was fashioned by the Creator, independent of my will, I cannot be responsible for that result, which I could not control. If the gentlemen who amuse themselves in this *noble* way can derive either pleasure or profit from the indulgence of such desires, I regard the liberty of the Press as the key-stone of that arch upon which our glorious constitution reposes in security; and I will not lightly question the extent of that liberty because envy, folly, or even a viler passion may stimulate a blockhead to violate the purity of such a privilege.

> " I have the honour to be, sir,
>> " Your obedient servant,
>>> " ROBERT COATES.

" 34, Craven Street, Strand,
" December 11th, 1811."

This plain-spoken letter did not meet with any reply from those whose articles had called it forth; but we desire our readers to become better acquainted with certain points to which it refers. As regards Mr. Coates selecting the *Morning Herald* for his letter, that paper was the acknowledged organ of the fashionable world at the period, and notably that of Carlton House; and as a large number of those who witnessed the performance and annoyance at the Haymarket Theatre belonged to the fashionable world, it was only wise to place the letter where it was most likely to meet their view.

With regard to the reference made to the trial of " Macklin *v.* Leigh " and other persons for rioting, Lord Mansfield, before whom the case was tried (the detailed report of the trial appears in Vyner's Abridgment), stated that a British audience had a right to express their approbation or disapprobation of plays and actors in the usual way; but if it could be proved that any person or persons went night after night to the theatre for the purpose of preventing an actor from exercising his profession,

or to injure the management or proprietors, such person or persons would
not only be subject to an action at law,
but might be indicted for the offence;
and in the case of the prisoners in the
King's Bench, Lord Mansfield stated that
if the parties concur in doing the act,
although they were not previously acquainted with each other, it is a conspiracy. The magistrates and managers
of Covent Garden Theatre during the
O.P. Riots in 1809, circulated the above
decision by placards and handbills, with
a view to deterring those bent on annoying
the actors and management.

With respect to the caricatures complained of, the allusion would have been
better unmade, as the very purpose of
such things is to portray an individual
with his person and features distorted,
leaving a sufficiency of true delineation
to identify the subject. As a fact, Mr.
Coates had no such unpleasing features
and figure as the complaints in his letter
would suggest. His stature was rather
above the medium, and his figure was

well proportioned ; though his features might be deemed somewhat austere, they were not unpleasing, particularly when animated ; his hair and whiskers were dark, which somewhat heightened the sallow tinge of his skin. These traits, coupled with his extraordinary taste for dress, could not but make him a somewhat attractive personage. Owing to his almost tropical birth he naturally felt the variability of the English climate in a marked degree ; so much so, that he was frequently to be met with either walking or driving enveloped in a coat or wrapper lined with costly furs.

Having seen many of the caricatures noticed by Mr. Coates, the writers can only say that they were satirical etchings, as so intended, and differ much from the miniature by Newton and the engraving by Blood.

A picture, presumed to be by Dewilde, of Mr. Coates as " Romeo," was humorously described by Charles Mathews the elder, with whom Mr. Coates was on intimate terms, although the actor sometimes " took

off" the amateur—this we shall notice in
another chapter. The work in question
s chronicled in "The Catalogue Raisonée
of Mr. Mathews' Gallery of Theatrical
Portraits"—(250)—Robert Coates as
"Romeo." "Here's to my love—Eyes
look your best." Act V. "As an amateur
became celebrated for his acting the parts
of ' Lothario ' and ' Romeo ' at the Haymarket."

Nor must we forget to mention, while
on the subject of personal appearance, the
partiality displayed by Mr. Coates until a
somewhat late period in life for blue
surtout coats, handsomely ornamented
with frogged braid, and a high shirt
collar, around which was worn a bright
and richly-coloured Bandana handkerchief.
His legs were encased in well wrinkled
Hessian boots, whose tops were adorned
with large tassels. The above was his
ordinary dress for walking; although, as
he advanced in years, he discarded his
magnificently braided coat, and eventually
the other marked attributes this fashion,
coupled with age, in a manner compelled.

In alluding to Mr. Coates' raiment, the papers of the day could not help trying to cause a little mirth at his expense ; one said (under title of " Army Clothing ") :—
" It having been reported that Mr. Coates was to be added to the Board for designing the new and foreign dressings, we are called upon in candour to contradict it, and to declare there never was the least ground for such an imputation on the ability of the present inventors."

CHAPTER IV.

Some account of the Baron de Geramb—Dedication
of *The Dramatic Censor* to Robert Coates—
Marriage of Miss Tylney Long, March 14, 1812
—Mr. Coates' second performance at the Theatre
Royal, Richmond, in the character of "Lothario,"
by request of H.R.H. the Duke of Clarence, and
for a charitable purpose—Miss Euphemia Boswell
and Mr. Coates.

AMONG the notabilities mentioned in the
preceding chapter, as being present upon
the occasion of Mr. Coates' *début* at the
Haymarket, was the Baron Ferdinand de
Geramb, of whom a short notice may be
à propos. This personage was of French
birth or extraction, and served in various
foreign armies. That in which he obtained
the most notoriety was the Austrian;
and he ultimately attained the dignity of
Chamberlain to the Emperor during his
sojourn in Austria. It is stated that he
married the widow of a rich Hungarian

noble *and assumed the title* of the lady's
former husband.   During the time he held
office in the Austrian Empire he appears
to   have   obtained   some   reputation   for
bravery by the rescue of a man drowning
in the Danube.   An account of this feat
appeared in the *Court Gazette,* as follows :—

" Presburg, Aug. 26, 1806.

" On the 21st of this month, at 7 o'clock
in the evening, a workman belonging to
this place inadvertently   fell into the .
Danube.   On seeing him fall and hearing
his screams, an immense crowd of persons
soon assembled, but no one amongst them
attempted to rescue him.   No boat was
handy to send to his assistance.   Every
other means threatened inevitable death to
those who had bravery enough to undertake the man's rescue, as the Danube (in
consequence of the very heavy rains) over-
flowed, which, particularly in this part,
added to the rapidity of the current.   At
this critical juncture, the Baron Ferdinand
de Geramb, actual Chamberlain of Service to
His Majesty the Emperor of Austria—who

is so renowned for his many and exalted
actions, and who in the last war raised the
regiment of Her Majesty the Empress,
which he conducted before the enemy—
now appeared at the sight of the unhappy
sufferer to fly to his relief by plunging
himself into the waves, without even un-
dressing. This was but the work of a
moment, and after a short interval the
Baron was plainly perceived, with the unfortunate he had saved, evidently struggling
against the strength of the torrent, till at
length, aided by an inimitable courage and
dexterity, he brought the man safe on shore.
In addition to this exemplary action, not
content with having saved the man's life,
he likewise made him a handsome present.
He further ingratiated himself with his
fellow-officers and comrades in the Austrian
army, by erecting a monument to the
memory of the Austrian Generals, Palsay,
Piazeck and Hotze, on the battle-field upon
which they so gloriously fell. The Baron
had, whilst in Palermo during the year
1807, an *affaire d'honneur* with a military
officer of high rank, based on a rather

curious agreement, to the following effect. The meeting was to take place on the summit of the volcano, Mount Etna, and that if either of the combatants fell, the crater was to become their tomb. The Baron's opponent escaped this novel burial by being put *hors de combat* at the second discharge of pistols, with a fractured arm, whilst his ball passed through the Baron's hat."

During 1810 the Baron de Geramb made overtures through our Ministers abroad, to be permitted to engage some 24,000 Croatians for service in the English army. To discuss this question more fully, Mr. Bathurst, General Oakes, and Mr. H. Wellesley granted him passports to prosecute his journey to this country for the purpose of seeing the authorities at the War Office thereon. Upon his arrival, accompanied by servants in gorgeous liveries, he soon became a prominent character at the West End, especially in the Park, where he appeared in a handsome vehicle, which displayed his singularly tight-laced, gold-braided and bedizened uniform to perfection. Nor must we omit to mention his enormous hirsute appendages in the form of a large pointed moustache, together with a fine pair of whiskers, which it is affirmed the Prince Regent was envious of and imitated. Howbeit, very soon these appendages, together with the tight-laced coat, became the fashion; and the originator of these was one of the most favoured guests at Carlton House, where his opinion was eagerly sought by its occupant on matters of dress, both for private and military purposes. One of the results of the latter appears to be the picturesque Hussar uniform, first worn in the British army about this time. From the notice he received from the Prince, the Baron very soon became one of the lions of the day, and was met with at every fashionable ball and rout, where he displayed amongst his other well-known attributes a pair of gold spurs several inches long. Thus courted and fêted, the purport of his advent seems to have been prolonged as much as possible, until it reached some twenty-two months in duration; when, towards the end of March, 1812, the neighbourhood of Bayswater, where the Baron resided, was excited and the curiosity of the passer-by arrested by a large poster affixed to the top of the house in which he dwelt. Upon the poster was printed the following, "My house is my castle: I am under the protection of the British Law." The cause for this remarkable placard was, that a warrant from the Secretary of State's office had been issued, under the Alien Act, for his apprehension; on which he refused to surrender, barred himself in and hung out the ultimatum before mentioned. The parties entrusted with the execution of the warrant at once applied to the Marlborough Street office for assistance. Messrs. Harrison and Craig, who were deputed to assist, returned with the messengers to the Baron's residence and again called upon him to surrender; but he refused, stating that he had 200 lbs. of gunpowder in the cellar, and that if they persevered in their efforts to dislodge him, he would blow them and himself up.

Nothing daunted, the officers now at-

F

tacked the garden gate, and forced it with hatchets; whereupon the Baron resigned himself peacefully, on the officers stating they were not *Bailiffs*. The Baron was lodged in the Bridewell at Tothill Fields till the following day, when he was conveyed in a post chaise and four to Dover and from thence shipped on board a vessel to Hamburg.

The reason for the above action on the part of the Government was, it is said, the discovery of some correspondence of a very compromising nature between the Baron and persons in Sicily; also that he was getting very troublesome by making extortionate demands on the Government. The latter were importunately made and not unfrequently accompanied by threats : therefore the Government deemed it necessary to act as they did. The account he furnished to the War Office for his services was as follows :—

Journey from Cadiz to London, 250*l*. Establishment in London twenty-two months, at 200*l*. per month, 4400*l*. Return to Hungary, 700*l*.—Total, 5350*l*.

Upon his landing at Hamburg the Baron thought fit to celebrate in verse the brilliant fête he had witnessed the previous year at Carlton House; introducing the names of certain members of the dethroned French dynasty, to whom he wished a speedy restoration. This being shown to the Emperor Napoleon, he showed his appreciation by ordering the Baron's arrest—although on neutral ground—and shut him up in the Château de Vincennes, where he was detained, fearing each day to be his last.

Having now time for reflection, he vowed that, should he ever regain his liberty, he would lay down the sword and enter a monastery. This desire becoming fulfilled, he turned Trappist, and entered the community of that Order near Reiningen in Alsace; and in time became Abbot and Procurator-general, wrote several works, and died March, 1848, at the age of seventy-six.

About the commencement of the year 1812 a book appeared, entitled "The Dramatic Censor, or a Critical and Bio-

graphical Illustration of the British Stage"
for the year 1811 inclusive, involving a
correct register of every night's performance at our metropolitan theatres : published with a view to sustain the morality
and dignity of the drama : edited by J. M.
Williams, LL.D.   This work was dedicated
to Robert Coates, Esq.   The following
is a copy of the dedication :—

"Sir,—As you are a distinguished
amateur of the Drama, and a primary
volunteer in the service of the Muses, I .
beg permission to transcribe the following
annual volume or Dramatic Register to
your protection ; and I feel emboldened
to say, that it is as honest an exposition of
the present state of our theatre as ever
was permitted to be published in this
metropolis by the agents of a misguided
authority.

"I have the honour to be, sir,
"Your very obliged servant,
"J. M. WILLIAMS.
"Feb. 1st, 1812."

This Dr. Williams was far better known

by his *nom de plume* Anthony Pasquin, and
was thoroughly in keeping, so far as his
writings usually went—if not in person—
with the Roman cobbler of that name, which
Dr. Williams assumed. The real Pasquin
flourished towards the end of the fifteenth
century; his stall or shop stood near the
Braschi Palace. Pasquin was famed for
his bitter remarks and caustic sayings;
these his namesake indulged in when he
felt disposed; in fact, many actors and
actresses, towards the close of the last
century and at the beginning of this,
received nothing but censure from
him. He was the terror of provincial
actors on their making their first appearance in London, and some curious instances of his conduct are on record,
quite unnecessary to dilate upon here.
That this person had talent none can
gainsay. His " Children of Thespis " and
other writings show him to have been a
man of some attainments and reflection.
He was also an engraver, having learned
that art under Bartolozzi; likewise a
painter, and had for some time at the

end of the preceding century been
amanuensis to a nobleman, who at one
time possessed the finest private theatre
ever owned by an amateur actor, and
whose taste for the drama was as pronounced as that of the subject of this
memoir.   Dr. Williams, although well
educated, and at one time under the
patronage of an earl who moved and
entertained in the highest circles, was
exceedingly careless and negligent about
his clothing and his person.   Possibly
Dr. Williams, although one of the most
severe theatrical critics of the time, had
keener wit than many of his *confrères*,
and knew the difference of a representation
by an amateur from that given by a professed actor; also his connection with the
noble amateur just mentioned may have
made him more lenient to the deficiencies
of a theatrical novice.   Be that as it may,
it is a fact that he reviewed the acting of
an amateur in a far wider spirit than that
generally shown in those days.   There
were those who suggested that he held the
same position with respect to Mr. Coates

as that he had filled in his late noble
employer's household, but this was not
true ; Mr. Coates having rendered him
simply the same assistance as he had
afforded to many others connected with
the stage, and which Dr. Williams needed
at one time. The before-mentioned work,
edited by Dr. Williams and mentioned a
few pages back, was, as its title implies,
a critical record of the various performances during the preceding year ; many
of these criticisms are in Dr. Williams'
peculiar style. Whether the book was
deemed superfluous after the exhaustive
newspaper reports which then appeared in
the daily papers, or whether the price
(16s.) was prohibitive to its circulation,
it is not possible to say ; it was not published another year.

On March 14th, 1812, at St. James's
Church, Piccadilly, the marriage of Miss
Tylney Long, whom we mentioned in a preceding chapter as being worshipped by so
many suitors, amongst them Mr. Coates,
took place. The favoured suitor was the
Honourable William Wellesley Pole, M.P.

for Queen's County, and Chief Secretary and Chancellor of the Exchequer in the Ministry of Ireland. This peculiarly fortunate young man—whose person and slender estate was preferred before the richest and most noble in the land—was a grandson of the Earl of Mornington; his father, who was at a later period created a peer by the title of Lord Maryborough, was the elder brother of the great Duke of Wellington, uncle to the Hon. Wm. Wellesley Pole, who acquired by his marriage, not only a charming and accomplished wife, but the richest heiress in the country, together with one of the finest mansions in the kingdom, of which more anon.

A magazine of the time describes the wedding-gown as being of real Brussels point lace—the design was a sprig—draped over a skirt of white satin. The bride also wore a cottage bonnet of the same rich lace with two ostrich feathers; a deep lace veil and a satin pelisse trimmed with swansdown. The gown cost 700 guineas, the bonnet 150 guineas, and the veil 200 guineas. The lady's jewels consisted principally of a necklace and ear-rings of brilliants, the former cost 25,000 guineas; 800 wedding favours were distributed, worth 1½ guineas each, besides others of an inferior quality and price.

An odd circumstance is said to have attended the wedding. On the arrival of the happy pair at the hymeneal altar, the bridegroom was applied to by Dr. Glass for the ring, but he had forgotten to procure one. A messenger was in consequence dispatched to a jeweller, who immediately attended with an assortment of rings, and then the ceremony proceeded without further interruption.

Wanstead House, Essex, the ancestral home of Miss Tylney Long—who by her marriage became the Honourable Mrs. Wellesley Pole—was situated in an historical domain. Mention is made of it having been granted at one time to the Church of Westminster by Alfric, whose grant was confirmed by Edward the Confessor. According to the Domesday survey it was held by Ralph Fitz-Buen,

and since that period it had passed through
the hands of the Lords Rich, Robert, Earl
of Leicester (who entertained Queen
Elizabeth at this place, and married the
Countess of Essex, who, upon the death of
the Earl, married Sir Christopher Blount),
and through this family the estate passed
into the Earl of Devonshire's hands. In
1606 it escheated to the crown, and
King James in the following year passed
some time hunting in its park. The property passed shortly after into the possession of George, Marquis of Buckingham,
being subsequently purchased by Sir Henry
Mildmay and his wife, whose descendant,
Sir William Mildmay, sold it to Sir Josiah
Child. The latter was succeeded in the
estate by his son, Richard, afterwards
Earl Tylney, who in 1715 erected the new
mansion of which we are now speaking,
upon the site of the former edifice. This
nobleman's grandson dying in 1784, without issue, the Manor, together with other
large estates, devolved upon his nephew,
Sir James Tylney Long of Draycot, Wilt-
shire, where the family had been settled

for many generations. Sir James T. Long's only son, James, succeeded to the title and inheritance in 1794, but being a minor, his seat was let to the Prince de Condé. The youth we have just named died in his 11th year, and all this vast property devolved upon his sister, the subject of these few pages.

The mansion at Wanstead, standing in an extensive park, was a very large and magnificent structure. The front was 260 feet long; the entrance in the centre being beneath a grand portico of six Corinthian columns, having a flight of steps on each side, and in the tympanium the arms of the Tylney family finely sculptured. The architect was the well-known Colin Campbell, who received great praise for the science and judgment displayed in this work. The great hall, fifty-one feet by thirty-six, was decorated and furnished with all the splendour of the last century; the ball-room, seventy-five feet by twenty-seven, was magnificently fitted up, and the dining-room and saloons were furnished with corresponding taste and luxury. Most of the ceilings in the grand apartments were painted by Kent, a portrait of whom hung in the hall. The mansion also contained some fine paintings, among these were a Raphael, a Coreggio, and a Lely, also several by Cassali and other eminent old and new artists. The grounds contained a curious and interesting grotto, constructed by the second Earl Tylney, which cost some 2000*l*. to erect, independent of materials.

Such is a brief account of the principal seat of the wealthy heiress who by her marriage bestowed all these vast possessions on the object of her choice. Would anyone present at the nuptials of this couple have been bold enough to predict, would any necromancer have foretold, that in ten years, the bride's fine fortune would be squandered and gambled away by her husband, her estates mortgaged and sold, the mansion at Wanstead dismantled and disposed of, finally razed to the ground, and its materials dispersed? But we are anticipating the course of events.

During September, 1812, Mr. Coates made his second appearance at the

Richmond Theatre, in the character of the " Gay Lothario." Here again we have to record the fact of an overcrowded house, a critic of the time stating that no actor had ever been honoured with such full houses since Garrick's time. Even the pit was occupied by the beauty and fashion of the neighbourhood, who were unable to obtain seats elsewhere. The piece appears to have been well rendered and the characters ably sustained by the various actors, Mr. Coates sharing in the general applause; one or two of his passages with the love-lorn Calista were well received, and his rencontre with Horatio in the second act, elicited frequent bursts of applause.

During the interval between the play and the farce, Mr. Coates recited one of his favourite monologues, " The Hobbies," which was duly praised.

The object of this performance was of a twofold character. Firstly, to serve a charitable purpose, presumably on behalf of some disciple of the Muses in embarrassed circumstances. Secondly, for

the pleasure of H.R.H. the Duke of
Clarence, who had expressed a wish
through the medium of Lord Arthur
Hill, to see Mr. Coates in the character
of "Lothario." Thus the benevolent
purpose of the performance was doubly
enhanced by the presence of his Royal
Highness and his suite, for whose
pleasure, as well as that of Mr. Coates,
Lord Shaftesbury solicited the attendance
of Colonel Smith and some officers of the
10th Dragoons. The management, to
prevent a recurrence of the scene at the
Haymarket Theatre, secured the presence
of Lavender, the police officer; but
fortunately for the nobility and gentry
forming the greater portion of the
audience, as well as for the convenience
of the actors, the malcontents were
present in so small a number as to be
scarcely worthy of notice. Possibly many
who went to the theatre to annoy the
amateur every time he appeared, were
prevented by the large number of places
applied for by those in the vicinity so
soon as it was whispered about that Mr.

Coates would give another representation of "Lothario," at which H.R.H. the Duke of Clarence would be present. So numerous, indeed, were the applications for seats, that Mr. Beverley, the manager, was urged to let the gallery at box prices; but this he declined to do, stating that it would be trespassing too much upon the privileges of the play-going public. All the seats usually booked having been secured, Mr. Beverley, as well as the recipient for whom the performance was first arranged, and who would benefit after the deduction of the expenses for the night, had little cause for complaint upon the score of empty benches.

The Duke of Clarence appears to have been well pleased with Mr. Coates' efforts on this occasion; and his brother, the Duke of York, was, at an earlier period, much devoted to amateur theatricals, having himself played the part of "Lothario" upon more than one occasion. We cannot conclude the notice of this evening's entertainment without remarking how much better Mr. Coates played his

part when allowed to do so with comparative quietude; no doubt encouraged
by an appreciative audience, who applauded, not only his efforts to procure
their amusement, but those feelings which
prompted the representation.

In mentioning the subject of the
annoyance Mr. Coates so frequently met
with on the stage, we may add that he
knew perfectly well the originator of these
disturbances; although this person may
have been absent himself, he deputed
others to attend and create noise. We
are speaking now more particularly of
the first appearance of Mr. Coates at the
Haymarket, not that this was by any means
the only effort of this organized clique
to disturb and annoy the amateur. We
do not purpose to even hint at the identity
of the leader. Mr. Coates and his friends
well knew who it was, but as the first-
named performance was given for his own
pleasure, and when repeated nearly always
combined with a charitable object, he had
little or no redress, unless an actual assault
or breach of the peace was committed.

Shortly after the second appearance of Mr. Coates, he was applied to by Miss Euphemia Boswell, second daughter of James Boswell the biographer of Dr. Johnson, for some assistance which doubtless Mr. Coates had his reasons for not bestowing. As we have been unable to find or obtain a copy of the letter containing the request, we do not think it would be doing justice to Mr. Coates' memory to record, verbatim, his reply. That the letter asking the favour contained some allusions to Mr. Coates' position in society as well as to his means, is indicated by the character and tone of the reply he wrote. The letter was shortly after published by a satirical magazine, which continually derided the subject of this memoir. We fear that the letter, as well as the application, was not altogether the outcome of Miss Boswell's mind. The general tenour of Mr. Coates' answer was, that having some heavy demands to meet in a few days, he must be just before being generous; that were he to consider every

application he received for money he
would very soon be penniless; and also
that having already lent a large amount,
which he reckoned to be an absolute loss,
he had for the present left off being a
lender. Now comes the portion of the
reply that must have needed reflection,
and which no doubt was alluded to by
Miss Boswell in her letter. " If any
evil-disposed persons should endeavour
to impose on you, or insinuate this, that,
or the other, about my indulging in
theatrical representations, or the society
I may move in, they are welcome " ; and
he concluded by inviting Miss Boswell to
refer his traducers to the Treasury, his
agents and stockbrokers, and his bankers,
Messrs. Thomas Coutts and Co., who
would no doubt give them information
as to his character, means and position.
To this was added a suggestion that as
he, Mr. Coates, believed Miss Boswell's
brother to be a man of fortune, why had
she not first applied to him, who would,
he thought, relieve her wants, did he but
know of them.

Shortly after the receipt of this reply, Miss Boswell acknowledged it by the following, a portion of which we give :—

" I have received your letter. I do not repent of having applied to you as a supposed devotée of the stage : *au contraire*, as it would have been doing you an injustice not to have put it in your power to aid one of its disciples. I shall have you to add to the list of my nominal patrons, but should have been more gratified by having had it in my power to add you as a real one in the hour of need.

" I am, your obedient servant,

" Euphemia B. Boswell.

" P.S.—I shall thank you to send me the copy of lines I wrote for you to send to Miss Tylney Long !   I am urged to publish them.   The want of liberality in my affluent brother gives me a greater claim to the protection of strangers.   You had a brother also unkind, had you not ? (?) Is it true you are to stand for Westminster ? "

G 2

The foregoing letter shows unmistakable signs of irritation, in the demand for the return of the lines and the threat to publish them. But there can be no doubt that if Mr. Coates had called in Miss Boswell's services for this object, some corresponding return had been given for them. Furthermore, as the lady for whom the poetry was intended—whom Mr. Coates thought fit to approach in this manner, more in vogue then than at the present day—had been married, as we have previously recorded, in the March of this year, and Miss Boswell's letter or reply to Mr. Coates' refusal was not written until the following October, we fail to see how the publication of this sonnet could have harmed either the lady for whom it was written, or Mr. Coates, otherwise than by letting the world know that all the poetic effusions he addressed to Miss Tylney Long were not his own. But in this respect he would not have been singular, as many have used the same means, when desirous of approaching the object of their regard.

In respect to the remark of " the want of liberality in my affluent brother," most people will think with Mr. Coates, that it was Mr. Boswell's duty to assist or make provision for his sister, and not to leave her to the protection of strangers, which Miss Boswell suggests must be her lot, because of his irresponsibility. The allusion to Mr. Coates' unkind brother is not a happy one, seeing that all his sisters and brothers died in childhood. As for the suggestion that Mr. Coates was to stand for Westminster, it was a mere idle *canard*, no doubt intended to draw forth a second letter from Mr. Coates ; but we cannot trace this *ruse de plume* as being successful.

As many of our readers would like to see the lines mentioned above, we append them.

" Titian, could he but view thy heavenly face,
In vivid colours he'd each beauty trace.
Lucretia's charms were great, but thine surpass
Nature's first model—o'er that Grecian lass.
Enchanting fair one ! save, oh ! quickly save,
Your dying lover from an early grave.
Lady, ah ! too bewitching lady ! now beware
Of artful men that fain would thee ensnare,
Not for thy merit, but thy fortune's sake,
Give me your hand—your cash let venals take."

No doubt the suggestion for these verses was given by Mr. Coates, who was certainly prophetic in his forebodings, while his own admiration appears to have been disinterested.   The correspondence before mentioned occurred some time during September and October, 1812, and on the 5th of the December following, the Prince Regent bestowed on Miss Euphemia Boswell a Civil List pension of 49l. 10s. per annum, presumably for the services rendered to literature by her father.   A chronicler of the events of these times, Lady Charlotte Bury, notices this grant in her diary, which appears in the edition by Galt, 1838, Vol. iii., page 197 :—" I hear the Regent has given a mad daughter of James Boswell a pension, she is insane and very unworthy in many respects." These remarks are by a woman on a woman.   How far they are correct we will not venture an opinion ; suffice it to say that Miss Boswell lived for some time to enjoy her annuity.

CHAPTER V.

DURING the year 1812, many *fêtes* and
rejoicings were held. Two of the most
prominent were the *fêtes* given in honour
of the Bourbons at Carlton House, and
the depositing in Whitehall Chapel of the
standards taken from the French in Spain.
In fact, London was *en fête ;* and amongst
others who privately celebrated these events
was J. W. Elliston, the actor and lessee.
To show his appreciation of royalty, whose
favour he had long enjoyed, he gave an
entertainment at his house in Stratford

Place, to a select number of his own and Mrs. Elliston's friends, so Mr. Raymond, his biographer, informs us. Mr. Coates was one of the guests, as also were Dr. Kitchener, Mr. Phipps, Mr. Pope—a happy trio, and well able, with the aid and concurrence of their excellent host, to bring out the humours or idiosyncrasies of their fellow-guests. They were not long in bringing their arts to bear upon Mr. Coates.

Dr. Kitchener called upon him for a recitation, suggesting that as music was a sister art he would accompany the recitation with appropriate airs on the piano, which was agreed to. But the Doctor, no doubt being in a playful mood, made the tender passages in the scene between " Calista " and " Lothario " (which was the subject of Mr. Coates' recitation), unhearable by a very pronounced *obligato* instead of *pianissimo*. This caused much laughter, in which Mr. Coates joined; and after finishing his part observed, " That many great actors were frequently wanting in that nice discrimination which often marred some of their finest efforts. For himself he claimed indications of delicacy in recitations, etc., that neither Booth, Garrick, Kemble, or Barry ever exhibited: for instance, when I address Providence I always raise to myself the left hand—the innocent inoffensive limb— the right arm being the instrument of war and destruction."

"True," replied Mr. Pope, "but is it not also the hand of fellowship?"

"Ay, ay," laughed Mr. Coates, "but I myself am ambidexterous."

His host here intervened, and gave his guests a *bon mot* of Mr. Coates', which gained some applause.

They were speaking together of the merits of a certain great actor when someone observed, "That gentleman is beyond all praise."

"Yes," replied Mr. Coates, "so far beyond, that it will never reach him."

January 11th saw the second appearance of Mr. Coates upon the boards of the Theatre Royal, Haymarket. The piece selected for representation was as previously, Rowe's tragedy of *The Fair Penitent*, the amateur's favourite play at this time; and it was given on that evening for the benefit of a Mr. Sims.

The house was crowded to its utmost capacity soon after the opening of the doors; the lovers of Mr. Coates and novelty filled up the lobbies, and to obtain a seat was considered peculiar good fortune, after, however, a scene of conflict. The box-keepers, with the most praiseworthy and fruitless fidelity, endeavoured to keep the places previously booked for their rightful owners, but they were powerless against the torrent of eager sightseers, who rushed in and soon secured and held every seat in the house, and afterwards amused themselves by laughing at the discomfiture of the *bonâ fide* holders, as well as making the usual discordant noises so well-known to old playgoers.

The piece was better received than when the amateur first sought the suffrages of the stage-loving public, who doubtless thought that they must not be over-critical; though the papers which pub-

lished an account of this representation
were as unlenient as ever, not only to Mr.
Coates, but also to the portrayers of the
characters of " Altamont " and " Horatio."
This piece was followed by a farce called
Raising the Wind. Between the acts
Mr. Coates was to recite " The Hobbies."
The noisier part of the audience who had
come solely to see the amateur, did not
appear to understand this, and soon after
the conclusion of *The Fair Penitent,*
began to call lustily for " The Hobbies."
To such a pitch did the fever of impatience
rise, that " God save the King " was
played as a palliative to the feelings of the
audience, but without avail. The curtain
now rose for the farce, but all was dumb
show, not a word could be heard beyond
the cries for " The Hobbies ! " " The
Hobbies ! " until after repeated attempts
to gain a hearing, one of the actors stepped
forward and said that Mr. Coates would
give his recitation as mentioned in the
play-bills so soon as he had changed his
attire, after the first act of the farce.
This statement somewhat allayed the

tumult, but little notice was accorded to the stage. When the curtain fell, Mr. Coates came forward, attired in a scarlet military coat and a hat with a regulation feather. Bowing to the house, he requested pardon of the ladies for appearing without boots and spurs—his nether garments being knee-breeches, silk stockings, and shoes of the character he had just represented. He then gave the audience in a spirited manner that which they had called for with so much acclamation. "The Hobbies" was received with marked approbation. The farce was then allowed to proceed, but the audience rapidly thinned when they found Mr. Coates would not appear again that evening.

Mr. Coates made his third appearance at the Haymarket Theatre for the benefit of a widow. The play was *The Fair Penitent*, and the character sustained by Mr. Coates—"Lothario." The amateur was received with the usual cries from the occupants of the pit and gallery; but the interruption was not of sufficient force to stop the progress of the piece.

Some of the critics displayed the customary antagonism to the personifier of " Lothario "; nor were the other actors and actresses less harshly dealt with. Doubtless the latter were not perhaps those who did the utmost justice to their parts. The lady who played "Calista" is mentioned by one writer as " a thin, fantastic figure, who floated about with singular velocity, very different from the line of grace, and whose voice was less substantial than that of a disembodied spirit." This lady, he suggests, was Mrs. Coates, an observation which does not reflect credit on the writer's knowledge of his subject, seeing that Mr. Coates was at that time a bachelor and continued so for many years after; neither was the object of his later choice an actress, or in any way connected with that profession. This is only one of the numerous misrepresentations purposely made, concerning this gentleman, which appeared in the prints of the period, and, in fact, throughout the amateur's histrionic career.

At the conclusion of the play Mr. Coates made his appearance before the curtain, attired in a military jacket and cap, and gave his usual monologue, "The Hobbies," which the denizens of the pit and gallery as heartily applauded, as they had eagerly annoyed the actor in the play, making great efforts to secure an encore, which Mr. Coates, after the evening's labours, declined.

The house, as usual, when Mr. Coates performed, was crammed in every part; this was, no doubt, very gratifying to the person for whom the distinguished amateur's services were given.

Mr. Coates, on the 1st February, 1813, was presented by General Baker to the Prince Regent, at the levée held by him on that date, and was most graciously received by His Royal Highness. Mr. Coates had long cherished a desire to be numbered among the select friends of the occupier of Carlton House, but this wish was not gratified. We think he was really better known to their Royal Highnesses the Dukes of York and Clarence than he was to the Prince Regent. Perhaps it was as well for Mr. Coates that he did not gain the desired *entrée* amongst the chosen few. He was already well acquainted with some of their number, and frequently seen in their company either walking or driving in the Park in his well-known curricle, attended by two grooms, who used to stand at the heads of the horses while its owner, or a friend, entered or alighted.

Mr. Coates having been duly presented at Court, he was in no way surprised at receiving, on the morning of Thursday the 4th of February, 1813, a portentous missive sealed with the Royal arms, and left, so the attendants stated, by a "gentleman" in a scarlet coat. To open the packet and read its contents was but the work of a moment. It ran thus,—

"The Lord Chamberlain is commanded by His Royal Highness the Prince Regent to invite Mr. Robert Coates to a ball and supper at Carlton House on Friday evening. The company to appear in the costume of the manufacture of the country. Hour of attendance ten o'clock."

The above was written on a highly-finished card, to which was attached the usual Royal Heraldic Insignia. Mr. Coates naturally regarded the invitation as the outcome of the favourable notice he had received from H.R.H. the Prince Regent on the day of the levée; and gave orders for his diamonds to be polished and his wardrobe to produce its choicest apparel to do honour to so illustrious a host, the prince of connoisseurs, as well as of the Realm.

The time for his departure having arrived, Mr. Coates left his apartments in Craven Street a blaze of splendour; diamonds of the first water flashed on his bosom, whilst those on the hilt of his sword and upon his fingers, radiated with equal brilliancy. Having taken his seat in the chair prepared for his conveyance, he proceeded to his destination accompanied by two footmen in the most superb and costly liveries, reaching Carlton House in good time and without difficulty.

Upon this evening Colonels Bloomfield and Congreve were in attendance. The

first-named allowed Mr. Coates to pass
unchallenged, but on his presenting the
card of invitation to the latter he was informed with the utmost politeness that it
was a forgery !

Mr. Coates, upon hearing this, was in
no way put out, treated the affair with
apparent indifference, and begged Colonel
Congreve, who naturally felt some embarrassment on account of the disappointed
guest, not to trouble himself on his behalf,
or to acquaint his Royal Highness at the
moment with the circumstance. He made
his bow and retired, finding of course
that his chair and servants had gone
home.

As he emerged from the entrance he
was addressed by a well-muffled person,
who inquired why he had left ere the entertainment had commenced. Mr. Coates,
not recognizing the voice, replied that
there had been some little informality and
that he was on his way home, but that he
should first ask the Chevalier Ruspini's permission to view from his balcony, almost
directly opposite Carlton House, the arrival

H

of the remainder of the guests, which he did.

Mr. Coates' interrogator upon this occasion was the inimitable Theodore Hook, the perpetrator of the Berners Street Hoax; who, having obtained possession for a few hours of an authentic card of invitation to the Prince's fête, and being an excellent imitator of handwriting, deemed it a good opportunity to make fun of Mr. Coates. It is even asserted that he borrowed a military coat and plumed hat to deliver the missive at Mr. Coates' residence, doing this with all the air and swagger at his command.

Colonel Bloomfield acquainted the Prince Regent with the circumstance the next day. His Royal Highness was extremely indignant with the liberty that had been taken in his name; and urged that it would have been wiser not to have pointed out the fabrication to Mr. Coates, or to have refused admission upon its detection; further adding that the person to whom the evening's entertainment had been denied was an inoffensive gentleman, whose presence possibly might have amused very many of the guests, and certainly could have harmed none. The Regent recognized that had Mr. Coates been admitted, and informed of the circumstance afterwards, the perpetrator of the joke would have been outwitted, and the laugh have been at his expense, and not at that of his victim.

His Royal Highness, in order to give further proof of his deprecation of the matter, despatched his secretary next morning to apologize for the disappointment Mr. Coates had received; which, had H.R.H. been informed of the occurrence at the time, would not have been inflicted; likewise to desire Mr. Coates to come and view the decorations and arrangements made for the fête, which were still intact.

Mr. Coates warmly thanked the bearer of His Royal Highness's gracious message, and requested him to convey to the Prince his thanks for the kindness he had displayed, and to say that he would be much pleased to view the preparations that had been made for the entertainment of the honoured guests, of whom he had " almost " been one.

Whether Mr. Theodore Hook was reprimanded for the part he played or not is not known, but the joke was seldom after told by him without some show of compunction.

On February 10th 1813, Mr. Raymond held his benefit at the Theatre Royal, Drury Lane, upon which occasion *The Devil's Bridge* was performed, and *Honest Thieves* at the end of the opera. The bill also announced, " The Celebrated Amateur of Fashion " (for this night only) will recite " Bucks, have at ye all." As this can scarcely be called a performance, we pass it by without remark, except that no doubt Mr. Raymond claimed for Mr. Coates' presence the certainty of a full house, which would much enhance his looked-for gains of that evening ; nor was he disappointed.

On Wednesday, February 24th 1813, Mr. Coates again appeared as " Lothario " at the Haymarket Theatre (this being his

fourth appearance at that house), for the
benefit of the Widow Cherry and her
children. No sooner were the doors
opened than the rush began, and it ceased
only when every point of view was
occupied, either for sitting or standing.
Then, as usually, the wags and malcontents
there assembled amused themselves until
the hour fixed for the commencement of
the play with crowing, neighing, etc.,
etc.; performances no doubt as amusing
to these proficients as it was annoying to
the audience assembled to see Mr. Coates
as an amateur actor. Upon the curtain
rising, Mr. Waldegrave of Drury Lane
Theatre, who played "Horatio," and a
Mr. Elkington who played "Altamont,"
presented themselves to address the
audience, but the noise was so great they
could not be heard. Mr. Carr of the
Theatre Royal, Drury Lane, who appeared
in the character of "Sciolto," next
essayed to address the house, and after
patiently waiting some minutes obtained
a brief period of silence, which gave him
time to say, "Ladies and gentlemen,

we are the regular servants of the public, and perform this evening in aid of the widow and orphans of a man who was warmly esteemed by many, and respected by all that knew him." Here the noise began again so loudly that the trio withdrew to make room for Mr. Coates and the commencement of the play; immediately on presenting himself, he was greeted with loud applause, accompanied by the other noises before mentioned. The piece was not allowed to run smoothly owing to the frequent disturbances caused by those on mischief bent, and to whom the purport of the representation was of small moment, if any, so long as they could roar themselves hoarse and get up a fracas, if possible, against a gentleman amateur who was striving to benefit the distressed and indigent. Nor were the malcontents amongst the audience the only ones who strove to mar the easy working of the piece; for one of the trio who had come forward upon the raising of the curtain to announce the objects of their appearance nearly brought the performance to an abrupt termination by his misjudged remarks. "Horatio" was the character this person was sustaining; and, in the second act he should say, in taunting "Lothario," "When you are met among your set of fools, talk of your dress, of dice, or horses, and yourselves; it's safer, and becomes your understanding better." For *horses* "Horatio" substituted the word "curricles," which raised such a clamour that for nearly a quarter of an hour not a word could be heard. Mr. Coates upon hearing this personal allusion started back with indignation, and then advancing a pace or two, in apparent agitation, to the front of the stage, attempted to obtain a hearing, but in vain. He then went towards "Horatio" as if to ask the meaning of the insult offered by his departure from the text. Others say that the exact transgression of the actor was as follows,—

"Why drive you in state about the town
With curricle and pair—your crest a cock "—

"Horatio" now endeavoured to speak, but his efforts were as futile as those of

Mr. Coates had been, whereupon he left the stage. A short lull having now succeeded the deafening noises, Mr. Coates spoke as follows:—

" Ladies and gentlemen—I was solicited to play for a lady who I was informed was an object deserving of attention. (Applause.) I further beg leave to state that there are several performers in this place who belong to our great theatres, and let me add that one of them has taken a most unwarrantable liberty with me. Many of you may have doubtless read the play of *The Fair Penitent*, and, if not, you may do so to-morrow, but there you will find something about horses and merriment. But a performer has no right to endeavour to hurt my feelings by inserting allusions to me not in his part. Let my equipage be laughed at by those that choose; my father, who left me a large fortune, wherewith I indulge my whims, likewise taught me good manners. I am little given to boasting, but if I may be allowed to say a few words on my own conduct, I can say I consider myself a most useful character; for, if my dress be extravagant, and my equipages expensive, let it be remembered it is this that supports the working-classes. Does it not assist the tailors, mercers, and coach-makers? In these respects I set, what I think, a laudable example."

This speech was received by the audience according to their views of the case, some applauding, whilst others yelled and crowed to their heart's delight. The latter, we may assume, were the avowed opponents of the amateur.

The gentleman playing the character of " Horatio " came forward and said he had already assured Mr. Coates that he meant to give no offence, and he now, upon his honour, disclaimed any such intention. This apology was deemed satisfactory, and Mr. Coates, after consulting some friends in a stage-box, generously came forward and shook hands : thus ended an incident that might have caused considerable trouble. The play then proceeded without further interruption.

At Covent Garden Theatre, on February

25th 1813, a two-act farce called *At Home*, written by Sir Henry Bate Dudley, was produced. The *dramatis personæ* were:—

Captain Dash . . .	Mr. Liston
Mr. Raymond . . .	Mr. Blanchard
Mr. Neville . .	Mr. Farley
Mr. Drill . . .	Mr. Emery
Emily (Daughter of Mr. Raymond) . .	Miss Booth
Lady Dancy (Her Aunt) .	Mrs. Davenport
Romeo Rantall . .	Mr. Charles Mathews
Sir Oliver Oldboy .	Mr. Simmons
Jenny	Mrs. Simes
Housekeeper . . .	Mrs. Findlay.

A strong cast for this trifle, which has a very simple plot.

An adventurer, Captain Dash, is captivated by Emily, an heiress, and the daughter of Mr. Raymond. In order to effect an elopement the Captain gives an assembly, which he styles his " At Home," and at this an amateur dramatic performance or recitation is to take place. On this occasion he seeks an opportunity of enticing Emily into the grounds where a post-chaise is in waiting. Before, however, the Captain can put his plans into operation, Mr. Neville—Emily's real lover

—causes him to be arrested during the festivities, at his suit for a debt of 100*l*. he had previously lent him. Knowing the Captain to be enamoured of his *fiancée*, and seeing the chaise in the grounds, he immediately divines its purpose, and at once seeks out Emily, acquaints her of the narrow escape she has had, and prevails on her to use the vehicle for their own elopement. This they do, during the confusion consequent upon the Captain's arrest. Amongst the visitors is one, Romeo Rantall—impersonated by that then peerless mimic, Charles Mathews the elder—who is asked to exhibit his dramatic powers. To this demand he consents. Mr. Coates was the object of this malignant satire : his manner, dress, and idioms were very correctly imitated, and the mimic, as Mr. Coates had done at the Haymarket on his first appearance, shook hands with a gentleman in the stage-box.

On this evening the effect of that incident was considerably heightened by Mr. Coates himself being present in the stage-box, and his impersonator, Mr. Mathews, as "Romeo Rantall," coming forward and shaking hands with him.

Some of the critics asserted that this was a previously-planned affair, but it was merely a coincidence ; Mr. Coates having heard that his friend Mr. Mathews was going to give a representation of himself, curiosity led him to witness the farce, with the result above related.

It is said that Mr. Mathews made more of the character than the author intended, chiefly dwelling on a favourite phrase "You know," and reciting the following monologue :—

"YE FAIR, AN AMATEUR."

Ye fair, an amateur before you view,
Whose love of tragedizing sprang from you ;
Upon my love-sick soul it's very true.
Your soft-blown sighs he trusts you'll now decree
That he an unique actor still may be :
Sighs that must waft his woe-enchanting name
High on the play-bills of theatric fame.

Strutting, while the company applaud.

But, ah ! If cruelly you should deem it meet
To tread his tragic buskins under feet,
He must submit, alack ! a well a day,
And throw his diamond dagger far away.

Ye dimpled dears, if for smiles you'll not be wooed,
He'd rather win you to a melting mood.
Call forth these things in lily white array
When pearls of pity from your eyes would stray.

Unfolding a white handkerchief.

I keep a hobby, prattling folks declare,
And ride him oddly, just to make folks stare.
A frisky hobby, as you all well know,
When bitted up for gay Lo-tha-ri-o.
And yet he lets, with mighty little trouble,
Undone Calista ride behind me double.

Advancing, amidst plaudits, and shaking hands with a person in the box.

To trust no brother coxcomb I'll incline ;
To cut the comb of cocks high game is mine ;
But let them proudly in their tragic pen
Crow ! strut ! and peck — peck, strut and crow
    again !

Most of the journals which published
theatrical criticisms took great objection
to this form of ridicule ; and one of
them, which usually lost no opportunity
of maligning the Amateur, was constrained
to conclude its account of the representation with the following pungent remarks :
" But still the principle is most repre-
hensible, and the idea of ' taking off '
living characters upon the stage, which
has been abandoned till now since the

days of Foote, is likely to be productive
not only of quarrels and canings among
individuals (with which we should have
no fault to find), but of contentions and
disturbances at places of public resort,
which every advocate for order and
decency would wish to be avoided. In
every point, therefore, 'At Home' is
despicable; it is despicable on the stage,
despicable in writing, despicable in con-
ception, and despicable in principle, and
that it reached its second night is the
grossest libel on public taste and
judgment." With all its strong cast of
characters the farce could not keep the
boards for more than twenty-five nights,
a clear public rebuke to the author and
management. The public, it is fair to
assume, liked to witness Mr. Coates'
theatrical efforts in his own person and
not by deputy. The audience several
times during the run of this piece grew
weary of Mr. Mathews' overdoing of his
part, and cried " Off, off! " a cry that must
have been somewhat novel to him.

CHAPTER VI.

Mr. Coates appeared for the fifth time at the Haymarket on March 1st 1813, and gave one of his favourite monologues. The entertainment was got up for the benefit of a certain Lady Perrott, who, for many years, had been afflicted with serious illness. The piece on this evening was *Othello*. At the conclusion of the play, the curtain again rose to find Mr. Coates sitting at a table upon which was wine ; filling a glass from the decanter, he walked to the footlights and good-naturedly " drank to the health of his enemies, whom he desired might live to see him prosper." This ebullition of kind feeling was received by the audience with loud cheers and applause; after which Mr. Coates proceeded with his recitation, and was more than patiently heard; indeed, the audience demanded an encore. After a long solicitation, Mr. Coates appeared again, but only rendered the first half-dozen lines, bowed respectfully and retired. Upon this the calls for his reappearance were louder and more prolonged than ever, but no inducement could bring the Amateur forth again that evening.

On April 26th 1813, Mr. Coates' services were again requested in aid of a benefit for Miss FitzHenry (daughter of Lady Perrott), a lady who occasionally appeared on the stage—principally at Bath, where she had had short engagements. The theatre selected for the representation was again the Haymarket, (making his sixth performance), and the play *Romeo and Juliet*, in which Mr. Coates sustained his old character of

" Romeo." Long before the overture
was given by the orchestra it was
impossible to obtain a seat; and when
the curtain rose it was difficult to find
even standing room. The first act was
purposely somewhat shortened, but the
play ran very well, until Romeo and
Juliet are about to be married, when
clamour arose in the gallery. On the
finish of the scene where Juliet retires
—which character Miss FitzHenry sustained—she threw a look of withering
contempt at the gods, who resolved to
return a " Roland for an Oliver." Upon
her re-entering, the noise and shouting
from this quarter were terrific, some of
the occupants of the pit joining in the
uproar. The lady made ineffectual
courtesies and entreating gestures, but
to no effect. Some of the actors and
actresses upon the stage urged her to go
off until the storm had passed over;
this she declined to do, but clung to the
scenery and pillars in great agitation.
At last a lull occurred, when she came
forward and demanded to know what

I

there was in her character or in her conduct that night which merited their disapprobation. Mr. Coates, she urged, had kindly rendered his services for her benefit.

The rest of her address was made inaudible by another burst of uproar, mingled with shouts and groans, during which the lady withdrew. One of the actors now came forward and asked whether the audience were desirous that the play should proceed or not. Taking their answer to be in the affirmative, the performance went on without much interruption to its close; and thus ended this eventful night. Miss FitzHenry was much hurt at the unfeeling and unmanly conduct of the rougher element of the audience, and disavowed any desire to treat them contemptuously; she had merely wished to rebuke their unruly behaviour. She was, however, well satisfied with her benefit from a pecuniary point of view.

On May 10th 1813, Mr. Coates again appeared for the seventh time at the

Haymarket Theatre in his old character of " Romeo." We regret having to record that one of the most noisy houses assembled to witness this representation, also to annoy and vex Mr. Coates. In fact, a strong party had organized itself purposely for this occasion, and members of it were seated in groups in nearly every part of the house, which, as usual, was crowded in every part. On the appearance of Mr. Coates upon the stage he was received by this band of rioters with crows and laughter, together with many insulting epithets and allusions. These he treated with unconcern, and the play proceeded until the duel in which " Romeo" kills " Tybalt." No sooner had the combatants placed themselves in their respective postures of attack and defence than the house was convulsed with laughter by the appearance of a bantam cock strutting on the stage almost at the feet of " Romeo," at whom it had been thrown by one of the malcontents, who had obtained a stage-box for this purpose. Upon the laughter ceasing, one of the party shouted from another part of the house, "O most gallant Romeo, stain not thy sword with the blood of Tybalt, but kill the cock before you." This speech in the meantime caused another burst of laughter.

The harmless cause of all this hilarity was strutting about the stage preparing for a crow. In this, however, he, as well as those who had placed him there for that purpose, were disappointed; for, almost at the last moment, " old Capulet " caught him up in his arms and bore him off the stage. The yells that followed this act of "old Capulet's," who had thus deprived the party of disturbers of one of their most telling efforts, were ear-piercing, and in order to heighten their effect, the sides of the boxes were beaten with sticks, accompanied by a great clamour on a tin kettle in the gallery. In fact, the tumult was general, but nevertheless the play ran on, and "Romeo" killed "Tybalt," and made his exit, reappearing, however, at the side scenes opposite to the stage-box from which the cock had been thrown, and, showing himself just sufficiently for its occupants to see him, shook his sword, with which he had just been fencing, at them. This they resented, and called lustily for "an apology for shaking your sword," but the demand was not complied with. On the actors again appearing they were one and all pelted with orange-peel by the members of this *choice* band of rioters, and thereupon made a sudden exit.

One of the occupants of the stage-box endeavoured to address the audience from the stage, but they would not hear him. The well-mannered persons present now resented the interruption caused by the organized rioters. This person finding his efforts useless, returned to his box, only to come forth again directly Mr. Coates made his appearance, from whom he demanded an apology. Mr. Coates naturally declined to comply, and proceeded with his part. Now was the opportunity for those in the pit, who resented the behaviour of the rioters, to show their disapprobation of the conduct of one of their number, by assailing him in the same way as they had previously done the actors, viz., with orange-peel; this they continued to shower upon the demander of the apology until he beat a hasty retreat.

The play dragged wearily along without much further incident, until the scene in which "Romeo" kills "Paris"; when the latter, supposed to be lying dead on the ground, was suddenly aroused to life by a terrific blow on the nose from an orange. Determined, though presumably dead, not to be made a mark of, the actor started to his feet, pointed to the orange, and walked off the stage. This caused a further uproar, which, however, soon subsided. Mr. Coates and his fellow actors were permitted to finish the play; although the former was considerably annoyed during the tomb scene by shouts of "Why don't you die?" etc., etc. The curtain, having fallen on the last act of the tragedy, rose shortly after for Mr. Coates' reappearance to recite "The Hobbies." This, the organized band of rioters endeavoured to disturb, but not sufficiently to prevent its successful ending.

The object of this performance being charity, can anyone of the present day understand such indecorous and indecent behaviour on the part of a gang unfavourable to Mr. Coates ?. If they objected to his acting, more effectual resentment could have been shown by their keeping away. If Mr. Coates' performances were so bad, as their continued disapprobation and vexation would lead one to believe, why not have let him address empty benches instead of full ones ?   That the Amateur had a following, is demonstrated by the fact that the house was always packed whenever he appeared ; and the audience no doubt viewed his representation in the right spirit, as undertaken for charitable purposes, and judged him as an amateur. Besides, even had this gentleman been striving to earn his living on the stage, and to gain fame and fortune by his acting, there would have been no excuse for this scandalous treatment by a clique of persons, who attended most of his performances for no other purpose than to ridicule and annoy him.

On May 29th 1813, Mr. Eyre, late of Drury Lane, who was at this period in pecuniary difficulties, held a benefit at the Lyceum Theatre, and solicited and urged Mr. Coates to appear in the character of "Romeo" on that evening for his behoof. Mr. Coates having consented, the play-bill appeared as follows :—

THEATRE ROYAL, LYCEUM, by permission of the Lord Chamberlain, for the benefit of Mr. Eyre, who has the honour to announce to his friends and the public that by the generous and voluntary assistance of the united talents of the principal performers of the Theatre Royal, Drury Lane, and by the kind permission of the sub-committee of that theatre, will be acted on Saturday next, May 29th 1813, the tragedy of *Romeo and Juliet*. The part of "Romeo" by the celebrated Amateur of Fashion, who has liberally offered his support on the occasion.

Starved Apothecary	Mr. Knight
Peter	Mr. Penley
Prince	Mr. Gladstone
Paris	Mr. Crooke
Montague	Mr. Maddocks
Capulet	Mr. Marshall
Benvolis	Mr. Holland
Tybalt	Mr. de Camp
Friar Lawrence	Mr. Bennett
Friar John	Mr. Sparkes
Page	Miss Carr
Samson	Mr. Chatterby

Gregory   .   .   .   .   Mr. Evans
Balthazar .   .   .   .   Mr. Miller
Mercutio .   .   .   .   Mr. Russell
  (Late of the Theatre Royal and Drury Lane)
Juliet   .   .   .   .   Miss Bellchambers
(By the Theatre Royal, Drury Lane.   Her first
        appearance in this character)
Lady Capulet   .   .   .   Miss Tidswell
Nurse   .   .   .   .   Mr. Dowton

Preceding the play, the Dramatic Sketch of

"BLUE DEVILS."

Migun   .   .   .   .   Mr. Elliston
James   .   .   .   .   Mr. de Camp
Dennison .   .   .   .   Mr. Palmer
Annette   .   .   .   .   Miss Kelly

At the end of the play (by desire) A Yorkshire
        Recitation, called—

"RICHARD AND BETTY AT HICKLETON FAIR,"

By Mr. Knight.

In the course of the evening the celebrated song of
"The Woodpecker," by Mr. Braham.   A comic song,
called "The London Newspapers," by Mr. Bannister.
To conclude with a farce, called—

"HOW TO DIE FOR LOVE."

Baron Aldorft   .   .   .   Mr. Carr
Captain Blanfield   .   .   Mr. Wrench
Captain Thalewick   .   .   Mr. Russell
Trap   .   .   .   .   Mr. Knight
Quick   .   .   .   .   Mr. Oxberry
Michael   .   .   .   .   Mr. Maddocks
Charlotte   .   .   .   Miss Kelly

Doors opened at half-past five, and to begin at half-
past six.

Boxes 6s., pit 3s. 6d., first gallery 2s., second 1s.

This entertainment was not wanting on

the score of variety, irrespective of the amount of talent engaged in it. Mr. Eyre had, however, a narrow escape from a really serious dilemma, for at the ninth hour the lady who had promised to play "Juliet," and who was announced to do so in the bills, was unable to appear. Mr. Eyre, fearful of the consequences that the change of programme would entail as well as of probable loss to himself, managed to get Miss Sydney to sustain the character at a few hours' notice. During the play, Mr. Coates, as usual, met with interruptions from the galleries, but as they were not strong or prolonged they could not be said to disturb the harmony of the evening. Miss Sydney, for whose appearance on behalf of Miss Bellchambers a printed apology had been circulated throughout the theatre, acquitted herself, it is said, most ably. A critique on her performance said it could not have partaken more in look and manner of the genuine spirit of the author, or be more entitled to unqualified approbation.

The writer of this criticism accords

little, if any, commendation to Mr. Coates;
but it seems hard to believe that Miss
Sydney could have commanded the approbation she received for portraying tho
character of " Juliet " unless the person
playing " Romeo " upheld that part in
some way approaching to a good representation. A hopelessly bad, clumsy, and
careless actor would have rendered many
of her passages and actions futile.

The next record of Mr. Coates' appearance at a theatre is not as a performer on
the stage—although he sustained almost
as difficult a character as any other it had
been his lot to appear in, viz., that of a
peace-maker.

On June 1st, 1813, one of the most
serious fracas ever known at a place of
public entertainment occurred at the Opera
House. The performance announced was
Enrico IV., in which Madame Catalani
was to have played the leading part. The
bills of the evening simply announced that
" she had withdrawn herself from the
theatre," but the real reason was that the
manager had not paid her, therefore she

refused to appear,—not the only prima
donna who has done the same thing.
But the strangest action on the part of the
management was permitting the opera to
proceed *without any actress* taking the part
that Madame Catalani was to have sustained, which was one of the most prominent. Upon the audience seeing this,
they naturally regarded it as a great affront
to them. They had paid to hear the prima
donna, and here was a piece presented to
them with the principal character omitted,
without apology or substitute. The mur-
mured disapproval at length broke into
loud clamours so soon as the ballet, which
was received with hisses and groans and
calls for Catalani, commenced. The occu-
piers of the pit having been augmented, the
noise and disorder became more furious
than ever. At last one of the side scenes
fell upon the stage, whether by accident
or design is not known; but almost immediately afterwards there was further
commotion behind another part of the
scenery—this was said to be an actual
fight, and greatly alarmed some of the

corps de ballet. The soldiers on the stage tried to repress the disturbance and to prevent the combatants breaking forth; it however appeared that the persons they were endeavouring to force back were a number of gentlemen from the audience, who had gone behind the scenes to find the manager, and who at last broke in upon the stage by sheer weight of numbers. Their sudden appearance alarmed the occupants of the stage, and the invaders presented a most sombre spectacle on account of their attire being regulated by the general mourning. It was noticed that each of the invaders carried a cane, some had two. The performers, fearful for their own safety, withdrew to the back of the stage and left the attacking party in sole possession of the front. From this point of vantage they immediately began to beat and tear the lower part of the scenery and to destroy all that came in their way. Upon this scene of havoc the curtain at last fell; when other malcontents came before it and walked up and down, flourishing their canes, gesticulating violently, and waving branches of laurels, the spoils of the stage properties. The management, anxious for the safety of the curtain, now ordered it to be raised, and thus gave the roiters possession of the arena. Amid all this excitement there were continual calls for " the Manager," others vigorously applauded the invaders, whilst some as loudly cried " Off ! off! " At last a person appeared on behalf of the management, and was challenged by one or two indifferent speakers in the pit as to the reason for delay in appearing. The others demanded an apology to appear in every daily print for the misconduct of the management. To these requirements the individual bowed meekly, and endeavoured several times to gain a hearing, but with little effect. He was, however, understood to have said that it was impossible for Mr. Taylor (the lessee) to appear personally that night on account of his unfortunate situation. He trusted they would suffer the ballet to proceed, and possibly Mr. Taylor might be able to appear on Tuesday. Respecting Madame Catalani, he was very sorry that unpleasant difficulties had arisen, but he could only say that everything practicable should be done to satisfy the desires of the nobility and gentry. These remarks were received with some applause, but several of the ringleaders upon the stage informed him that nothing would be considered satisfactory short of the restoration of Madame Catalani ; others then called out for Angiolini. Nothing useful resulting from these proceedings, the deputy withdrew. Attempts were now made to clear the stage, and allow the ballet to proceed. The soldiers appeared for that purpose, formed in line, and endeavoured to repress those of the audience who had gained access to the stage. This was the signal for the latter to be strongly reinforced, and a most extraordinary scene ensued. An attack being made on the soldiers—who had become separated from each other—they were surrounded by numbers of the rioters and overpowered by sheer force. The rioters snatched away their arms and threw them into the orchestra and pit. This affair was watched with breathless interest by those of the audience who still retained their seats, and who were fearful of the safety of their fellows, thinking that a British soldier would not allow himself to be disarmed without a sanguinary encounter. This circumstance speaks highly for the cool conduct of the men on such a trying occasion, for, although resisting the efforts of the invaders to totally disarm them, they had the good sense not to give the fracas a tragic ending. The management then brought the soldiers from the front doors to reinforce their comrades; but the former not knowing the state of the case, appeared somewhat incautiously, whereupon they were immediately treated in the same manner as their brethren. The gallant wearers of the King's uniform, upon being conquered, withdrew in a body from the stage, leaving the invaders jubilant with victory. Some better-ordered persons from the audience now shouted "Off! off!" whilst others facetiously demanded "God save the King." At last some agitation was noticed upon the stage, and a circle was formed round a gentleman—said to have been Colonel Mellish—who wished to address the audience, but could scarce obtain a hearing. However, during the intervals of comparative quiet, he was understood to say " that his friend, Captain White—(this gentleman was in command of the military on duty that evening)—had disclaimed any intention to interfere improperly with the audience, adding that it was not to break but to keep the peace that the soldiers had been withdrawn on his (Colonel Mellish's) solicitation." He concluded his speech by remarks favourable to the majority, and upon its termination, he was loudly cheered.

Now followed a somewhat ludicrous scene; some of the beaus on the stage advanced to the proscenium boxes, and shook hands with the ladies seated in them, as though congratulating them on their victory, and bowed to those beyond reach in the same spirit. Everything now seemed *couleur de rose*, until one luckless member of the Beau Monde began walking rapidly up and down upon the stage,

K

at the same time gesticulating and utter-
ing silly remarks. This raised the ire of
the audience in the pit and gallery, who
shouted phrases and remonstrances which
raised the choler of the gentleman in
question, and he, to show his contempt,
turned his back to the audience in a
significant but vulgar manner. This
conduct could not be tolerated even by
his own friends on the stage, and they
immediately insisted on his apologizing
on bended knees. Declining to do this,
he was ruthlessly seized by many of his
former associates, and dragged several
times ignominiously up and down the
stage, until he was forced upon his knees.
Even then he would not make the demanded apology. Again he was dragged
along the floor, his coat was quite, and
his vest nearly pulled off; while his cravat
was dragged at each end until he was
nigh being choked. In fact, the usage he
received excited the pity of the spectators
as much as his previous conduct had de-
servedly merited their disgust. So many
were engaged pulling about this victim

of their resentment, that in the scuffle and haste several persons fell over the foot-lights into the orchestra, but their place was immediately taken by others just as eager to mete out punishment to the offender, so that the crowd on the stage was larger than ever. A gentleman in the audience (Mr. Kinnaird) having made some signs that he wished to speak, silence was with some difficulty procured. He made, with considerable force and energy, a statement to the effect that the "cause of the present confusion was much aggravated by the shameful and scandalous conduct of the individual then on the floor of the house, and who, it had been found, was in a state of inebriety." Many upon the stage here exclaimed that the person in question was not drunk, as he would not have been able to make so good a defence were he so. Many now shouted for the speaker to give the person's name. Mr. Kinnaird, continuing, said "that he did not know it; that he should have felt the knowledge of such as great a degradation as he had, with others, felt his presence that night."

The evening was now fast drawing to a close, and wanted but a few minutes to the hour of twelve, when another speaker appeared ; one who up to the present had been a silent spectator of this extraordinary riot, and who was none other than Mr. Coates. His presence having been noticed by several prominent persons in the audience, they asked him to use his best endeavours to pacify the turbulence. To this he consented, and speedily obtained silence on rising to address the audience. He began : " Ladies and gentlemen, it is a great misfortune, we must admit, to be deprived of the talents of Madame Catalani, but it is of no use for us to make a riot." Here the party on the stage thought their own action the correct one in the matter, and drove Mr. Coates off the stage ! With him many went and rejoined their friends in the boxes. The curtain now finally fell, as the hour was almost midnight. Mr. Coates, however, made another effort to speak from a form in the pit, and quickly gathered a circle round him. Continuing : " That he hoped some treaty would be entered into with Madame Catalani that her services might be secured, and that rioting could do no good, having seen the bad consequences of such acts during my acquaintance with the public theatres. Even I, who never intentionally offended anyone in my life, let them be of what country they might—except the Muses, and they were outlandish—assure you, ladies and gentlemen, that my services shall never be wanting for the public benefit," adding "that he deemed it wise, in such a tumultuous gathering as was just upon the stage, to walk off at the first instance of opposition, as one never knew what might happen in such an assembly, deeming it more prudent than insisting on a hearing." At the conclusion of these remarks, no one else coming forward to speak, the company dispersed. Thus closed an entertainment—if such it can be termed—which took place at one of the chief places of public amusement in the metropolis, amidst a scene of disorder and tumult that has not since occurred and, it is hoped, never will.

On December 1st, 1813, Mr. Coates

appeared for the second time at the Lyceum Theatre, and sustained a character that he had not yet attempted in London, viz., that of " Belcour " in *The West Indian.*

The purpose of the play was to benefit a Mrs. Bury, the wife of a subaltern in the army, then serving in Spain, who had become somewhat straitened in circumstances. Her endeavours to procure a livelihood by teaching music, in addition to what small portion of her husband's pay he could allow, having failed, she bethought herself of a theatrical entertainment to provide further funds for a time. Hearing the substantial benefits that had resulted to those who had been fortunate enough to induce Mr. Coates to appear on their behalf—every ticket having been taken by people eager to witness his performance—this lady (Mrs. Bury) therefore thought she could not do better than solicit Mr. Coates' aid. She waited upon him at his apartments; but, not finding him at home, made her business known to Mrs. Lyall, the landlady of the house. Here we shall relate the

proceedings of this night's entertainment
before giving the sequel of the interview
above mentioned.   Soon after the raising
of the curtain, a commotion was noticed
in the pit.   A young man there called out
that he insisted upon addressing the house
before the play proceeded any further;
and with this purpose he begged hard to
get a hearing.' Silence being obtained,
he made the following extraordinary statement, prefacing it by saying he had come
there perfectly unknown to Mr. Coates or
his connections; nor did he desire to
injure that gentleman in any way.   On
the contrary, he hoped that the present
opportunity would give Mr. Coates a
chance of wiping off a stain on his reputation, which he trusted from his soul was
produced by malignity and slander; should
this be so, he would be the first person to
give him support and applause.   He now
begged leave to lay before the house the
transaction which implicated Mr. Coates,
and in the way that it had been related to
him.   Here an interruption ensued by
cries of "Hear, hear! Bravo!" etc.

Resuming, he said, "Ladies and gentlemen, the charge against Mr. Coates is that
he does not act upon a principle of philanthropy, but directly or indirectly gives his
services for remuneration." "Where?
where? Prove! prove!" from all parts
of the house. "Ladies and gentlemen,
as the best way is to be brief, I will come
to the point at once. About the latter end
of April, a lady, the wife of a subaltern in
his Majesty's service on duty abroad, who
was in much straitened circumstances in
spite of every effort she could make to
improve her position by giving music
lessons, thought she would try and raise
some funds by a theatrical entertainment.
Having heard of Mr. Coates' generosity
in these matters, she applied to him,
through the medium of Mrs. Lyall, that
gentleman's landlady. Your surprise will
be as great as mine was, ladies and gentlemen, on learning that this aid was per-
sistently refused, through the same medium
as it was asked, until the bénéficiaire agreed
to *give Mrs. Lyall* 40*l.* for the Amateur's
services: 20*l.* to be paid by bill before the

performance took place, the other half
was never called for. I have, ladies and
gentlemen, professed myself Mr. Coates'
friend. I have proved this by bringing
this business forward, thus giving him an
opportunity of proving to the public
whether he is in deed and in truth a
philanthropic 'Amateur of Fashion.'"

At the termination of this indictment
Mr. Coates was so thunderstruck at the
charge made against him that he at first
thought it was a *ruse de théâtre* on the
part of another organized body of disturbers, to produce an uproar. To test
the feeling of the audience he appealed
to them, and asked that the person in the
pit " who prevented their peaceably attending to the play might be removed "; but
the cries of "Answer to the charge " soon
convinced Mr. Coates that the speaker
had excited the curiosity of the audience.
During the few minutes that had elapsed
since Mr. Coates addressed the house the
Amateur came from the back of the stage,
where he had been writing, and said,
" Ladies and gentlemen, I believe I am

now perfectly able to satisfy the person who has addressed you." He then read a paper to the following effect:—" I, Robert Coates, do upon my honour declare that I never did, directly or indirectly, receive money for acting, and that all the tickets that I have in the house are paid for.

"(Signed)   ROBERT COATES."

This paper was then handed round the house.

The person making the indictment said, in reply to this, that he hoped Mr. Coates was correct, but the bill for 20*l.*, which had been paid to Mrs. Lyall, was in his possession—here produced and read. Continuing, he desired any person who wished further information to obtain the same by waiting upon the lady, Mrs. Bury, who resided in Bolingbroke Row, Walworth. He then sat down, but this indictment quite upset the audience, whose opinions were for the time divided, leading to a confusion of cries each time the Amateur appeared on the stage, and continuing until the termination of the play.

We here append a copy of the Programme for that evening; and beg to call the reader's attention (1) to the bénéficiaire being termed a widow; this, as we have seen, was sailing under false colours; (2) to the foot-note, which was inspired by the scandalous behaviour of the organized body of rioters, who attended Mr. Coates' last performance at the Haymarket Theatre, where they pelted the actors with orange-peel, etc.

THEATRE ROYAL, LYCEUM.

(By permission of the Right Honourable the Lord Chamberlain.)

This present Wednesday, December 1st, 1813,
For the benefit of a Widow,
Will be performed Cumberland's much-admired Comedy of

"THE WEST INDIAN."

Stockwell	Mr. Moreton.
Captain Dudley . . .	Mr. Truman.
Charles Dudley . . .	Mr. Austen.
Falmer	Mr. Posette.
Sailor	Mr. Hardy.
Major P. Flaherty . .	Mr. Dennis.
Varland	Mr. Minton.
Stukely	Mr. Smith.
Servants	White and Dunn.

The part of " BELCOUR " by the PHILANTHROPIC
AMATEUR OF FASHION.

Lady Rusport . . .	Mrs. Ladbroke.
Mrs. Falmer . . .	Mrs. Richardson.
Charlotte Rusport . .	Miss Rivers.
Louisa Dudley . . .	By a young lady.
Lucy	Miss Cook.

The Original Prologue to be spoken by a gentleman
after the play. Miss Harrison, from the King's
Theatre, will dance her favourite Pas Seul, to which
will be added the farce of

"BARNABY BRITTLE."

Barnaby Brittle . . .	Mr. Grosette.
Clodpole . . .	Mr. Dennis.
Sir Peter Pride . . .	Mr. Smith.
Lady Pride	Mrs. Richardson.
Lovemore	Mr. Austen.
Jeremy	Mr. Minton.
Damaris	Mrs. Ladbroke.
Mrs. Brittle . . .	By a young lady.

The doors to be opened at half-past five, and the
performance to begin at half-past six. Boxes, 6s.;
Pit, 3s. 6d.; Gallery, 2s.; Upper Gallery, 1s.

N.B.—A Reward of 5l. will be paid by the gentleman who plays "Belcour" on conviction of *each*
offender throwing anything on the stage to annoy the
performers.

CHAPTER VII.

THE charge publicly brought against Mr. Coates, which we have just related, gave him great concern. Mr. Coates spared no trouble and expense to arrive at a solution of the matter.

It appeared that Mrs. Lyall, the landlady of the house in which Mr. Coates had his apartments, in Craven Street, had previously sought the Amateur's services for her own benefit, and that his aid was freely given. The performance was one of those we have recently recorded as given for the benefit of an unnamed "widow," and was held at the Háymarket Theatre with a highly satisfactory result.

This was, doubtless, the reason for Mrs. Lyall's course of action. She found so many persons ready to avail themselves of Mr. Coates' philanthropic services, and whom she waited upon when that gentle-man was from home, that the opportunity for obtaining a douceur or a final payment for bringing the wants of visitors under the notice of Mr. Coates, was used, as we shall see, to her own advantage, and to the mystification of the hirer of her apart-ments.

Having at last arrived at the truth of the matter, Mr. Coates was very angry, and demanded a full apology from Mrs. Lyall, to be accompanied by a sworn affidavit, incriminating herself, and ab-solving Mr. Coates from all participation in, or knowledge of, her nefarious practices. Failing this, he declared that he would adopt every legal measure to prove his innocence. His terms were at last agreed to *in toto*, with the following result :—

NOTE.

LONDON TO WIT.

" I, MARTHA LYALL, of 34, Craven Street, Strand, having heard it said that Robert Coates, Esq., late of Antigua, had participated in *monies given to this deponent* by Mrs. Bury, to induce the said Robert Coates to recite at Freemasons' Hall, at a concert given for the benefit of Mrs. Bury, certain verses written for the occasion, and, knowing such representation to be *untrue*, this deponent voluntarily maketh oath and saith that her receiving money to persuade the said Robert Coates to recite the last-mentioned verses, or to perform in public, was totally unknown to the said Robert Coates. And, this deponent, in her conscience, believes that if the said Robert Coates had known that this deponent had received any money from any person whatsoever, for the purpose of inducing the said Robert Coates to perform at any theatre, or recite verses in any public room, the said Robert Coates would not have consented so to do. And, lastly, this deponent positively saith that the said Robert Coates never did, in any way whatever, participate in any present given to this deponent by any person or persons to influence this deponent in persuading the said Robert Coates to perform, nor did the said Robert Coates ever know of this deponent having received any money from any person or persons, for whose benefit he had consented to play, until he was charged at the Lyceum Theatre with participating in money so received by the deponent.

"(Signed)   M. LYALL."

SWORN at the Mansion House, in the City of London, this 16th day of February, 1814, before me,

WM. DOMVILLE,
Mayor.

The foregoing affidavit appeared in several of the public prints of the period, and was a sufficient refutation of the charge heedlessly brought against Mr. Coates in a place of public amusement.

It is unnecessary to say that the charge

was not believed in from the first by Mr.
Coates' more intimate friends, but such an
imputation could not be made without
serious damage to Mr. Coates in the eyes
of society and the public generally unless
it was most strenuously denied, not only
by himself, but by the person of whose
nefarious action he was the unfortunate
victim.

That a charge of the kind may be
reiterated in after years, notwithstanding
the most ample refutation, is proved by the
fact that fifty years after this occurrence, a
writer of an article in a London magazine
—to which we shall allude later—refers
to the accusation without the slightest
reference to the refutation of it, which he
probably never saw.

However, this occurrence did not
prevent Mr. Coates' services being as
much sought after as ever by the necessi-
tous, but he was more careful in according
them. To show the public that he was
totally independent of the stage, he did
not appear as a performer at any of
the London theatres for some three

or four months after the affair at the Lyceum.

When he next presented himself before a London audience it was at the earnest solicitation of a lady for whose benefit he had acted the previous year, and who was relying on the kind support that he had formerly given so generously.

We must now allude to an incident that occurred towards the close of the Brighton season of 1813. Mr. Coates, as we have previously seen, had inherited a very valuable collection of diamonds, to which he himself added from time to time. Among other purchases, he ordered from an eminent jeweller a set of brilliant coat buttons, which he entrusted to his tailor for placing on a dress coat which he took to Brighton. It was some time, however, before a ball took place there of sufficient importance to authorize his wearing so extravagant and dazzling an article of attire. At last an opportunity presented itself, and Mr. Coates attended the ball, wearing this faultlessly-made and sparkling garment. All eyes were at once riveted on the glittering buttons. The ladies admired, and the gentlemen applied their eye-glasses; the coat and its wearer were the observed of all beholders, also the talk of the room. When the dancing began, Mr. Coates found that he had omitted to engage a partner, and for the moment every lady had her engagement-card full. Here was a dilemma! To stand in a ball-room without partaking in its gaiety, was not at all to Mr. Coates' liking; moreover, the effect of the refulgent buttons would be increased a hundredfold during the whirl of the dance.

Another visitor at length arrived in the form of a handsome young lady, who, through some detention, had been obliged to arrive late. Soon after her entrance, Mr. Coates asked her hand for a dance. The young lady declined, not wishing perhaps to accept the first beau that offered himself as a partner. After a short interval, Mr. Coates again advanced, and successfully renewed his solicitations for a dance.

By the commotion amongst the other

guests, so soon as they observed her
partner and self preparing for the
dance, the young lady readily divined
that she had procured the hero of the
evening as a partner, and resolved on
her course of action. During the dance
she observed to Mr. Coates that she was
sorry to have engaged herself to him,
as her attire was but plain compared to
the splendour of his habiliments; and
she could see that the assembled guests
were quizzing her on this account; therefore she requested to be allowed to retire.
To this her partner demurred, and
entreated her to finish the dance; but the
young lady became more determined as
Mr. Coates' anxiety to retain her as his
partner increased. They had almost parted,
when the Amateur made a further appeal,
to which she replied by saying she could
only consent to remain his partner upon
condition that he should present to her
one of the diamond buttons off his coat,
to wear in her hair as a sort of aigrette.
The situation was delicate, but there was
no other alternative for the moment; so he

produced a penknife, cut off one of the glistening buttons and fixed it in the lady's hair.

This adventure procured Mr. Coates great *éclat*, but was likely to be attended also with considerable cost to him, as other ladies present had their eyes upon the brilliant buttons for head-dress wear; so much so that Mr. Coates was afraid that, before he could get back to town, his coat would be shorn of its valuable appendages.

On the 28th February, 1814, Mr. Coates reappeared upon the stage of the Haymarket Theatre. This time, however, he did not sustain a character in any play, but recited. The person who had induced him to appear was Lady Perrott, whose benefit the preceding year had been so great a pecuniary success. Owing, doubtless, to the crowded houses ensured by Mr. Coates' appearance, she again solicited his aid, and this he promised to give in the manner just related. The house was well attended by an appreciative audience, for whose delectation Lady

Perrott had prepared the following sufficiently diversified programme :—

THEATRE ROYAL, HAYMARKET, by permission of
the Right Honourable the Lord Chamberlain, for the
benefit of Lady Perrott, who, recently recovered from a
long and dangerous illness, respectfully solicits that
patronage she most gratefully acknowledges to have
been honoured with by a generous public after eighteen
years of unparalleled sufferings.

This present Monday, February 28th, 1814,

"THE TRAGEDY OF TAMERLANE."

Tamerlane   .   .   .   Sir Edward Perrott, Bart.
(who last year performed Othello)
Moneses   .   .   .   Mr. Mortimer
Ascalla .   .   .   .   Mr. Merton
Prince of Tanais   .   .   Mr. Willis
Omar   .   .   .   .   Mr. Haswell
Mervan .   .   .   .   Mr: Hurst
Tama   .   .   .   .   Mr. Wright
Haly   .   .   .   .   Mr. Newton
Devise .   .   .   .   Mr. Denton

Bajazet (by the gentleman who some years ago performed Macbeth)

Selime .   .   .   .   Miss FitzHenry
(of the Theatre Royal, Bath)
Aspasia   .   .   .   Lady Perrott

The philanthropic Amateur of Fashion has kindly
consented to give his admired dissertation on
" The Hobbies."

The Castanet Dance by Miss Newcomb, who danced
on Mr. Webb's night.

A favourite Comic Song by a gentleman.

Mr. Wilson (late of the Opera House) will dance a
Nautical Hornpipe in character.
And, by particular desire, "The Tortoise-shell Tom-cat,"
by Mr. Marshall.

The whole to conclude with
"BON TON ; OR, HIGH LIFE ABOVE STAIRS."

Lord Minicken . : .	Mr. Wyatt
Jessamy	Mr. Dainby
Sir John Toottley . . .	Mr. Hewett
Colonel Tivey . . .	Mr. Smith
Davy	Mr. Doorish
Lady Minicken . . .	Mrs. Baker
Jym	Mrs. Haythorn
Miss Tittup	Miss FitzHenry

Boxes, 6s. Pit, 3s. 6d. Gallery, 2s. Upper Gallery, 1s.

The doors to be opened at half-past five, and the performance to begin at half-past six. Tickets to be had of Mr. Waud, confectioner, Bond Street ; Mr. Cruickshanks, perfumer, Haymarket ; Lowndes and Hobbs, printers, Marquis Court, Drury Lane ; and Mr. Massingham, at the box-office of the theatre.

In the issue of March 1814, of that scurrilous periodical the *Satirist*, a coloured double sheet engraving appeared, which portrayed Mr. Coates in a somewhat novel situation. The plate is named "Theatrical Faux Pas," and depicts a scene on a stage. Upon the left hand is a street door with the face of the Amateur grossly caricatured for a knocker, which is supposed to be saying, "Come live with me, and be my love!" On the right hand is a row of actors and actresses, making remarks, no doubt *à propos* to themselves and characters.

The explanation that accompanies the above, is as follows :—

"'Theatrical Faux Pas'—Mr. Satirist, I send you a farcical account of a farce lately privately performed, and a design for a caricature. If you think the subject worthy of winning the plate—there is a good deal of brass on it—which in my humble judgment would shine on copper; but that as you please. Print it or throw it on the fire; it is all one to your humble servant, A SCENE-SHIFTER."

Dramatis Personæ.

Drum on the Knocker . .	By an Amateur of Fashion
Altamont	Mr. Horrass
The Gallant Lobski . .	Mr. Fawcett
Charley Sputter . . .	Mr. Incledon
Crookmouth	Mr. Mathews
Beauty	Mr. Liston
Magister Moram . . .	Mr. Emery
Estifonia	Mrs. H. Johnson
Norvicia	Miss Stephens
Patagonia	Mrs. Liston
Betty Hunt	Miss S. Booth

This magazine was one of Mr. Coates' most bitter opponents during its brief career, and seldom lost an opportunity of making him an object of satirical effusions in prose or verse, as well as representing him on numerous occasions in cartoons. Howbeit, the Satirized outlived the *Satirist* by many many years.

About this period there appeared a pamphlet, entitled, " Report of the Extra-ordinary Trial of Charles Momus, comedian, for Stealing Property from the person of Romeo Lothario Doodledoo, Esq." By Jonathan Swiftsure, London, 1814. Price 1*s*. 6*d*.

This brochure was by Charles Mathews, who represents himself as Charles Momus, and was written as a sort of humorous defence of his impersonation of Mr. Coates as " Romeo Rantall," alluded to in a previous chapter, and which all the former's admirable and inimical vein of mimicry could not make a success. Mr. Mathews published this mock trial of himself as a sort of peace-offering to the offended critics and play-goers.

On the 7th March, 1814, Mr. Coates made another appearance as " Lothario " at the Haymarket Theatre. The perform-ance was undertaken on the behalf of Mr.

Sims, for whom he had appeared about
this time the preceding year, and who, like
Lady Perrott, again had recourse to his
services for securing an overflowing house.
Mr. Sims was again successful, though the
conduct of a certain unruly portion of the
audience who had come to annoy and
disturb the Amateur marred the occasion.
Mr. Coates, thinking doubtless that the
foot-note appended to the play-bill on the
occasion of his appearance at the Lyceum
would deter any organized body of disturbers when they found he intended to
take upon himself the punishment of those
who wantonly pelted and annoyed the
actors and actresses, had omitted to ask
Mr. Sims to put a similar notification on
his programme. It was evident, so soon
as the play began, that there was a strong
force of rioters present in all parts of the
house, who commenced the evening with
their usual senseless shouts and cries, to
the annoyance of the more respectable
part of the audience. The piece continued
until the scene where " Lothario " is killed.
This was the signal for the unruly persons

present to pelt the supposed corpse upon
the stage in the hope that he would be
forced to come to life again and beat a
hasty retreat, as a former actor had done
some time previously when Mr. Coates was
acting.   In this they were disappointed,
and Act 5 was played in a terrible uproar
caused by the enemies of order.   At the
termination of the play the Amateur was
so thoroughly disgusted with the indecent
behaviour of the malcontents that he left
the   theatre,   although   the   programme
announced that he was to give his favourite
recitation.   In   vain   did   the   audience,
friends and foes, clamour for his appearance ; their demands were made in vain ;
the object of their vehement calls could
not be found ; and thus he entered a silent
but effective protest against the disgraceful behaviour of the unruly members of
the audience.   It is stated that for at least
two hours, amidst the utmost confusion,
the house continued to call for Mr. Coates.
To make matters worse, during the progress of the *Fair Penitent* the gentleman who played " Horatio " brought down

the laughter and derision of the house by the misquoting of a sentence which should have been rendered, " Would I were a beggar and lived on scraps ! " Instead of this, the luckless wight said, " Would I were a baker and lived on sprats ! " With the non-appearance of Mr. Coates for his recitation the chief interest of the evening ended; the house could hardly have been said to notice the efforts of the other performers. We here append a copy of the play-bill for that evening, which was less varied than upon usual benefit nights :—

THEATRE ROYAL, HAYMARKET.
This present Monday, March 7th, 1814, will be presented
The Favourite Tragedy of the

" FAIR PENITENT "

Horatio	Mr. Anstin
Attamont	Mr. Worship
Lothario, by the celebrated Amateur of Fashion	
Calista . . .	By a young lady
(her third appearance in London)	
Lucilla	Mrs. Leftley
Lavinia (first time) . .	Miss Mortimer

After the play, a favourite " Irish Jig, " by Miss Smith from Dublin and a gentleman from the Opera House.

The spirited Monologue, written (?) by a bard of
Antigua, called

"A DISSERTATION UPON HOBBIES,"

will be recited in the character of a Hussar, by the
Amateur who plays " Lothario," in which he will
designate—The Courtier's Hobby, The Statesman's
Hobby, The Fiddler's Hobby, The Soldier's Hobby,
The Lady's Hobby, and His Own Hobby.   Two
favourite songs by Mr. Vernon ; to which will be
added a musical entertainment, called

" OF AGE TO-MORROW."

Frederick   .   .   .   Mr. King
(late of the Theatre Royal, Brighton)
Maria   .   .   .   .   Mrs. Henderson

The doors to be opened at half-past five, and the
performance to begin at half-past six.   Boxes, 6s. ; pit,
3s. 6d. ; gallery, 2s. ; upper gallery, 1s.   Tickets and
places to be had of Mr. Massingham, at the box-office,
where places may be booked from 10 till 4.

Lowndes and Hobbs, Printers, Magnus Court,
Drury Lane, London.

After the disgraceful proceedings of this
evening, Mr. Coates thought that however
much his appearance might benefit those
for whom he generously gave his services
(as well as being one of the most liberal
subscribers for tickets), it would be well
not to run the risk of possible injury for
their satisfaction, and determined in future
to contribute more freely in purse than in
person to the aid of those whom he

desired to benefit; although his own zeal, bordering upon eccentricity, for dramatic representations, was as great as ever. Even in later years, when age combined with a more careful judgment forbade his indulging in this cherished pursuit, he was still an enthusiastic play-goer and supporter of the drama.

But a fresh opportunity now offered itself to the Amateur for adding to his Thespian laurels. Many people in the country, having heard and read of his performances in London, were naturally anxious to see him in some of his favourite characters. This desire they communicated to the theatrical managers in or near the towns in which they resided. The managers were not slow in appealing to Mr. Coates' philanthropy, and at the same time they suggested appreciative audiences. To many of these solicitations he replied favourably, and arrangements were made regarding dates and the plays to be rendered. To give a detailed account of every appearance made in various parts of the country would be beyond the limits of the present work. We shall content ourselves by recording two or three of them; these may be taken as fair samples of the whole.

About the middle of September, 1814, Mr. Coates visited Birmingham for the purpose of performing " Lothario." The house was well filled, and the Amateur was graciously received upon his entrance by " The Brums," who heard him with attention. None of his old enemies were present to shriek and crow; on the contrary, he was greeted with loud and unanimous applause.

The tragedy proceeded without unusual incident except the rendering of several passages in a different way from that adopted by professional actors. The audience took the alterations in good part, on the whole, although there was some laughter, and all went well until the death of " Lothario," which produced a burst of applause from the audience, and cries of " Encore! encore!" This continuing, a novel scene ensued. The manager came forward and held a brief conversation with the *presumably dead* " *Lothario*," whom he *understood* to consent to the wishes of the audience. This the manager announced to the house, and the curtain fell, the audience expecting it to rise again on the solicited " encore " scene.

After the patience of many was exhausted, the curtain rose indeed, but for the last act, which was begun amid a general uproar, and repeated cries of " Encore."

As the noise continued, the manager had again to come forward and say " that he was sorry to have misunderstood Mr. Coates, who was willing to oblige the audience by speaking an address he had intended to have delivered before the Prince Regent and the Czar of Russia a short time back had the opportunity served, but would not enact the dying-scene again."

These remarks satisfied the audience, and the play was allowed to proceed. On its termination, the band played " See the conquering hero comes," and in marched Mr. Coates attired in regimentals. The house was hushed in an instant, but scarcely had the Amateur completed the first few lines than a wag in the gallery cried out "Sing it!" whereupon Mr. Coates, believing that a second misrepresentation had been made, walked off the stage, and no amount of inducements, bravos, and encores could make him return that evening.

The after-piece might just as well have been omitted, for not a word of it was audible.

On the 1st December, 1814, Mr. Coates appeared at the theatre at Stratford-on-Avon in the character of "Romeo," written, as the play-bill stated, " by that immortal bard Shakespeare, the pride and glory of Stratford ; and not only of Stratford but the British Empire. Mr. Coates will leave London for the express purpose of gratifying the inhabitants of Stratford and in honour of the birth-place of the great poet."

Charles Mathews the elder, in a letter to his wife, published by her in the Memoirs of her husband, humorously describes Mr. Coates' visit to Stratford,

M

which had just preceded his own. The epistle is sufficiently entertaining for us to give at some length :—

" Stratford-on-Avon,
        " December 24th, 1814.

" I finished here last night. Ha ! taken in completely : but I would not have missed my visit here altogether if it had been twice as bad. I thought, of course, there was a theatre here when I was invited to come over ; when I came—behold ! it was a barn, a miserable barn ! However, Bannister Dowton, Incledon, Mrs. Bartley, and others had acted here, and all for the honour of Shakespeare. So again I was content ; and the last first of December *that* ever *was* that darling Fancy's child of Nature—Coates—acted here, and was advertised in the character of ' Romeo.'

" After he had acted, he was determined to have a procession all by himself, a minor pageant or imitation of the Jubilee ; and walked, dressed as ' Romeo,' from the barn to the butcher's shop where Shakespeare was born. Here he wrote his name on the walls and in the book kept for that purpose, called himself the illustrator of the poet, complained of the house, said it was not half good enough for the divine bard to have been born in, and proposed to pull it down at his own expense and build it up again, so as to appear more worthy of such a being! He went to the church, wrote his name on the monument; and, being inspired, on the tablet close to the pen in the right hand of the bard, wrote, 'His name in ambient air still floats, and is adored by Robert Coates.'

" Dowton, too, kicked up a great dust in the house where Shakespeare was born. The old woman who shows it remembered him well; he must have been delicious. He desired to be left alone—'There go, I cannot have witnesses. I shall cry,— And so—eh! what? The divine Billy was born here, eh? The pride of all Nature has been in this room! I must kneel. Leave me! I don't like people to see me cry.' While alone, I suppose Shakespeare's apparition appeared and inspired him, for he produced the following couplet, which

M 2

appears on the walls, where there are 10,000 names, and 500 I think that I know amongst them :—

' With sacred awe I gaze these walls around
  And I tread with reverence o'er this hallowed
  ground.'

Bannister, too, went there after dinner, for the third time in one day, threw himself upon the bed in which the dear lying old woman swears Shakespeare was born—nay, shows the chair he was nursed in; but Jack threw himself in his drunken raptures on the bed and nearly smothered two children who were asleep, till his raptures awoke them. My own I must reserve for another letter—"

Mr. Coates having been well received, the manager solicited a second representation on behalf of some object or another, which was duly announced to take place on Saturday, the 3rd of December, 1814. A copy of the programme for that evening we here append :—

THEATRE, STRATFORD.

The birth-place of the Immortal Shakespeare.

R. COATES, Esq., the Amateur of Fashion, at the earnest solicitation of numerous ladies and gentlemen,

will perform the elegant character of "Lothario" in
the justly admired tragedy of the FAIR PENITENT,
having been honoured with the most distinguished
approbation in the character of "Romeo" on Thursday
evening by a brilliant and crowded audience.

On Saturday, December 3rd, 1814, will be acted
Rowe's Tragedy, called the FAIR PENITENT, the
part of "Lothario" by Mr. Coates. Positively the last
night of his appearing here.

Sciolto . . . . Mr. Frimbly.
Altamont . . . Mr. Morton.
Horatio . . . . Mr. Harding.
Rossano . . . . Mr. Morland.
Calista (the Fair Penitent) Mrs. Harding.
Lavinia . . . . Mrs. Morton.
Lucida . . . . Mrs. Lawrence.

At the end of the play "A Dissertation on
Hobbies," by the Amateur of Fashion. A song by
Mrs. Harding. A dance by Mr. Frimbly, Junr. To
conclude with, by desire, the laughable new farce of

"THE SLEEP WALKER ; OR, WHICH IS THE LADY ?"

Sir Patrick Maguire . Mr. Erwood.
Squire Rattlepate . . Mr. Morton.
Jorum . . . Mr. Harding.
Alibi . . . . Mr. Frimbly.
Thomas . . . . Mr. Frimbly, Junr.
Spy . . . . Mr. Parsons.
Sommo (the Sleep Walker) Mr. Kendall.
Susan . . . . Mrs. Morton.
Mrs. Dewram . . Mrs. Lawrence.
Sophia . . . . Mrs. Harding.

Doors to be open at a quarter after six, to
commence precisely at a quarter before seven, and
conclude by half-past ten. No half price will be
taken. Tickets to be had of Mr. Ward, printer.

Boxes, 3s. ; Pit, 2s. ; Gallery, 1s. J. Ward, printer, Stratford-on-Avon.

The proceeds of this performance were such as to satisfy Mr. Coates that he was thoroughly appreciated by the good people of Stratford-on-Avon.

CHAPTER VIII.

MR. COATES, it is said, had every reason
to be gratified by his reception in the
provinces, if we except the Birmingham
incident—and he resolved, like a warrior
of old, to rest upon his " renown " for a
while; not that he purposed to withdraw
himself from the beau monde, where he
was looked upon as a sort of lion, notably
at Lady Cork's. In fact, the Amateur
was not the person to hide his light under
a bushel; and he made a rule to enjoy
the good things of this life to the fullest
extent of his means. He was, however,
not given to any of the vices then fashion-

able, for his taste for theatricals, gaudy equipages and faultless steeds, diamonds, and dress can hardly be reckoned as a vice. Indeed, a high opinion of the personal character of Mr. Coates was entertained by those best acquainted with him. He scorned to adopt the ideas of life of some of his contemporaries, who at this time partook freely of his hospitality and borrowed his money, which in face of the cloud then hanging over West Indian Possessions, he would have been wiser to have husbanded.

Although Mr. Coates was seldom seen on the tragic boards during the year 1815 —a period occupied in celebrating the overthrow of Napoleon—he had not by any means forgotten or given up his long cherished " hobby," nor were his services unsought by needy and unfortunate sons and daughters of Thespis, whom he aided by his purse and frequent attendances at their performances ; but he persevered in his resolution to desist for a time from acting. Mr. Coates' friends and acquaintances at this time were legion.

Amongst other well-known characters

was the fashionable Viscount Petersham, afterwards Earl of Harrington, and ultimately husband of the celebrated actress Miss Foote, of Covent Garden. This gentleman was a "unique" dandy. Some say he at one time cut out his own garments, but it is certain that he was the originator of the long overcoat, named the "Petersham," which many old beaus may still remember. He was a great authority on the compounding of snuffs! hence that still known as the "Petersham" mixture. We must not omit to mention his skill in the tea-tasting line ; this, however, appears to have been one of his father's hobbies. By the judicious mingling of certain growths, he formed a blende so pleasing that a cup of tea at Harrington House was a fashionable privilege and institution. It is said, also, that the private room of this eccentric nobleman resembled a grocer's shop, being fitted up with shelves, upon which were placed jars of various snuffs, together with the well-known tin canisters containing almost every kind of the then-grown tea. Nor did his clothes, snuffs, or tea monopolize all his attention, for his boots and shoes were polished with a blacking of his own making, of which he was very proud. To these oddities he added singularity in the trappings of his horses, in the colour of his equipage and the style of dress worn by his servants; although in none of these did he rival in notoriety the peculiar vehicle of his friend Mr. Coates. Lord Petersham's equipage was remarkable for its excessive plainness, both carriage and horses being of a brown colour, and the harness of the latter of an antique pattern, while the servants wore long brown coats reaching down to their feet, and tall glazed hats with large cockades. This nobleman, as might be imagined, was a great collector of snuff boxes; he had one, it is said, for every day in the year.

Another friend of Mr. Coates was Sir Lumley St. George Skeffington, Bart., of Bilston, Lincolnshire, and Skeffington Hall, Leicestershire, where his family had at one time held large estates. Unfortunately his father's errors, coupled with his

own generosity in permitting the former
to cut off the entail, so curtailed his means
that he was unable to make the appearance in society necessary then as now to
secure eminence in the world of fashion.
This gentleman took a high place in Mr.
Coates' esteem, no doubt from the fact of
his being a devoted admirer of the stage ;
and at one time, no despicable amateur.
This led him at last into the paths of
literature as a dramatist. In fact, as a
schoolboy he showed a taste for poetry
and composition. His master having reprimanded him for not having performed
some Greek or Latin translations, immediately praised the youth next to him for the
elegance of his verse, which was in reality
the work of the former. At the termination of his scholastic career—during which
his performance of "Hamlet" and other
difficult characters, together with his
admirable reciting of poetry and epilogues,
etc., had rendered him famous—he entered
the full whirl of fashionable life, and for a
time bade his muse farewell. A few years
after, he resumed his former allegiance,

and wrote a comedy, which was produced at Covent Garden Theatre in May, 1802, entitled *The Word of Honour*. Its mere announcement excited much curiosity among fashionable people, who could not imagine that a man so essentially " about town " could find time to write; while those who knew him least deemed the venture a folly. His more intimate friends, including some of his old schoolfellows, were sanguine of his success. The night of the representation having arrived, one of the most brilliant assemblages ever gathered together at Covent Garden Theatre met to witness his comedy. It was received with overwhelming applause, and the author's success as a playwright was established. After this, Sir Lumley St. George Skeffington wrote many other dramatic pieces, as well as songs, poetry, etc. Some of the lines he addressed to Miss Foote and Madame Vestris are ardent and harmonious. Sir Lumley also enjoyed the reputation of being the most polished man of the time. *The Monthly Mirror*, a periodical of the period, said of him as follows :—

" Those who best know him declare that in point of temper he may be equalled, but not surpassed ; as to his manners, the suffrages of the most polished and polite circles in the kingdom have pronounced him one of the best-bred men of the present time, blending at once the *Vieille Cour* with the careless gracefulness of the modern school. He seems to do everything by chance, but it is such a chance as study could not improve. In short, whenever he trifles, it is with elegance, and whenever occasion calls for energy he is warm, spirited, and animated. Let it be further added, that he is a zealous friend and supporter of the drama and its representatives, evincing on every occasion an ardent inclination for the encouragement of merit.

It is also a fact well ascertained that he was never known to say, even in the most remote way, a disrespectful or unkind word of any person. In support of this there are many anecdotes of his politeness on record, but it is not our province to repeat them here. Eventually, this accomplished personage became engaged in litigation respecting some family affairs relating to what had once been their possessions. These involved him ultimately in such dire difficulties as to lead to a compulsory retirement to one of the then existent dismal Government " hotels " situated to the east of this city, where he sorrowfully passed his latter days.

A third intimate friend of Mr. Coates was as well known a character as either of the preceding, and on a better footing with the occupant of Carlton House than either. This person, Henry, the eighth and last Earl of Barrymore, had long enjoyed an unenviable notoriety. We cannot trace the origin of this intimacy between two persons so diametrically opposite in many respects to each other as Lord Barrymore and Mr. Coates, and must assume that it was the well-known friendship between the Earl and the Regent that probably induced Mr. Coates to keep on good terms with the former.

A small section ·of " Society," being influenced by the conduct of his antagonists at the theatres, amused itself at a private assembly where Mr. Coates was present by some of the despicable mystifications then in vogue and also in other allusions. Mr. Coates met these attempts at offence by good-humoured remarks; these however failed, and he ultimately left the room for a few minutes. Returning, he closed and locked the door, walked to the table, upon which he laid a case of pistols, and demanded at the same time satisfaction from the principal offender or an apology for his rudeness. The latter yielded at discretion, and an apology was immediately offered, to the satisfaction of all concerned.

The Amateur was excellent company, witty and amusing; he had the faculty of relating anecdotes with telling effect. One or two of these we here give :—

" *A Cheap Breakfast.*—Some gentlemen, breakfasting at an open window of one of the old-fashioned West End clubs, were disturbed by a *gamin* beseeching them for a pinch of salt. ' Salt!' said one, ' what do you want salt for ?' ' Boy,' replied another, ' you don't appear to have anything to eat with it.' 'No!' piteously replied the urchin, 'that is just my misfortune; but I hoped that if you gave me the salt, one of the other gentlemen would perhaps give me an egg or something else to eat it with.' The gentlemen were so well pleased by the boy's ready wit that they ordered him a breakfast from the kitchen at once.

" *The Rival Bootmakers.*—A squire from the Emerald Isle, desirous of having a pair of boots made to measure, went to the shop of a well-known disciple of Crispin who was a fellow-countryman of his own. Going to the shop shortly afterwards for the purpose of trying the boots on, he was displeased with their appearance and fit; and upon demanding an explanation from the maker, the latter stated 'That it was not his fault at all, at all! It's your honour's, bedad; for shure it's a big foot that you have, and what's more, an ugly one too!' This reply made the customer irate, and he refused to take the boots at any price. The next day the same person waited on a neighbouring knight of the 'Last,' who hailed from North of the Tweed, and asked him to take his measure; at the same time relating how he had been treated. The wary Scot applied his rule to the gentleman's foot, and remarked :—'I will not say that your honour has a big foot or a clumsy one, but it will take a deal of leather to make you a pair of boots.' This did not offend, and the Scot secured a good customer."

Mr. Coates being at Bath towards the close of the year 1816, the manager of the Theatre wished to obtain the favour of a representation from the Amateur either for his own or another actor's benefit, and desired Mr. Coates to appear as " Belcour " in the *West Indian*, a part he had not yet played at Bath. All preliminaries being settled, Mr. Coates appeared at the Theatre Royal, Bath, on the 14th of December, 1816; the parts of " Charles Dudley " and " Varlant " being respectively played by Messrs. Warde and Chatterley. The representation appears to have been exceedingly well received;

so much so, that Mr. Amateur Coates
was again solicited to appear. He consented to give two performances for the
manager's benefit if the latter would
place the proceeds of a third appearance
at the disposal of the committee of the
Pierrepoint Street Society, a charitable
institution of Bath. This being agreed
to, Mr. Coates played "Lothario" on
December 21st, 1816. Mr. Stanley
sustained the part of "Horatio," and
Mrs. W. West that of "Calista." The
evening's entertainment did not pass off
so quietly as the preceding, owing to the
conduct of an individual in the pit, who
stated—we assume on being privately
remonstrated with—that he bore no
personal dislike to Mr. Coates, but did
not care for his rendering of the character.
Rather a curious way of marking disapprobation, particularly when persisted in;
conduct which now-a-days would place
the disturber in the hands of the police.
The hissing being prolonged, the Amateur
appealed to the audience, saying: "That
he was going to appear one evening on

behalf of a charitable institution of that city, but if he was not permitted to go through his performance that evening without further annoyance and molestation he would not appear on the stage again. The person or persons who did not like his performance might have their money returned." This address put a stop to the opposition; the audience no doubt thinking it best that the dissent of the few should give way to the majority who were satisfied with the Amateur's exertions on behalf of one of their local institutions. This, it appears, Mr. Coates had himself selected as the object of his labours.

On the following evening the *Fair Penitent* was again acted, and on this occasion to a more patient and appreciative audience. At the termination of the play Mr. Coates repeated one of his well-known monologues.

The next evening, December 23rd, 1816, Mr. Coates played "Romeo" in the tragedy of *Romeo and Juliet.*

The bills announced this as follows :—

ROMEO, the philanthropic Amateur, Robert Coates, Esquire.

The profits of this evening will be placed at the disposal of the Pierrepoint Street Society.

The house was crowded, and the exertions of the actors were well received. Many present, who had witnessed Mr. Coates' first appearance on the English stage, thought him much improved, and attributed this to his London appearances.

We have already had occasion to record that Mr. Coates was burlesqued by Mr. Mathews in a farce called *At Home,* but omitted then to state that there was another piece in which allusion was made to the subject of this memoir. The piece is named *All at Coventry.* "Lively," one of the characters, says: "Ah! Romeo, my rum one, how are you?" "Eh! Why how the plague did you know me?" "Why, by your *Coates,* to be sure!" "Yes, they're the thing, ain't they? Diamond buttons—cost me 500*l.* apiece!"

CHAPTER IX.

THE appearance at the Theatre Royal,
Bath, in December, 1816, which we record
in the previous chapter, was almost the
latest of Mr. Coates' histrionic performances in plays upon the public stage,
though he frequently afterwards gave
recitations from plays, etc., in private, at
the houses of his numerous friends. The
Amateur gained more *éclat* by this means
than by his public exertions. The noisy
section of the play-loving public, as well as
those who purposely created disturbances,
could not forget Mr. Coates' curricle,
crest, and motto, while he was upon the

stage : these, they seemed to think, were a part of his individuality, and that he should never appear without them, so lustily were the crowing and the allusions to the curricle usually made. What should we think now, if an amateur of good private fortune made his appearance, drawing houses that even Garrick might have envied, and one who combined with dramatic taste that for unique and brilliant equipages — what would the present generation think of such a person being received with cries derisive of his armorial bearings, real or assumed, together with remarks upon his carriage and servants ? Would not such conduct on the part of any organized gang of disturbers be held guilty of utter want of decency and common sense, more especially if the representations were given gratuitously, and for a charitable purpose ?

The Slave Registry Bill, which had been introduced by Mr. Wilberforce during the Parliamentary Session of 1815, was regarded with dissatisfaction throughout the British West Indies. All the Houses of Assembly in the various Islands appointed Committees of their members to report on the measure, and those Committees reported that the Bill was promoted by a few fanatical persons utterly ignorant of the matter they undertook to legislate upon. Some went so far as to state that the Imperial Government had no right to legislate for the internal economy of the West Indian Islands.

During these contentions an insurrection broke out on April 14, 1816, amongst the slaves on certain estates in the Island of Barbadoes.

The slaves began the revolt by demolishing the houses of their overseers, and destroying the machinery used in the production of sugar, also by setting fire to the fields of sugar-cane. The news of this affair soon reached Bridgetown, the capital of the island, where the authorities proclaimed martial law, and despatched against the insurgents the troops and militia left at their disposal. The slaves fled to various parts of the island upon

the military approaching, but some of the
number unfortunately made a show of
defence, ultimately with the total loss of
some 800 or 900 killed and wounded,
besides a large number of prisoners.

Peace being restored, it was found that
at least some eighteen or twenty estates
had been ravaged and destroyed by the
insurgents. The loss of the owners was
further augmented by the number of
slaves killed and wounded during the
suppression of the revolt, and these losses
were increased by the execution and
imprisonment of others upon trial for
their share in the conspiracy. On the
other hand, it is only just to admit that
many negroes remained faithful to their
masters, some even defending them
against the attack of the insurgents.

About the 24th of April, General Sir
James Leith issued a proclamation to the
black population, setting forth the error
of their notions concerning the new
Registry Bill, and requesting them to bear
their lot peaceably. Almost the whole
body of West Indian proprietors attri-

buted this outbreak to the influence of the proposed Registry Bill on the minds of the slave population, who imagined it to be almost a law of general emancipation, the delay in granting which had aroused their fury.

The bad effects of this episode were felt over the whole body of islands forming the West Indian Possessions. Some of the Governments issued notices stating that they believed some delusion had been practised on the credulity of the most ignorant portion of the slave community by designing persons, who intimated that the Imperial Government had suggested their desire to the legislature of the different islands, that changes should be made in the condition of the slave population almost equal to total emancipation.

This the notices denied, stating that the Imperial Government were always willing to second the views of the Governments of the West Indian Colonies for the amelioration of the condition of their slaves, but beyond this no interference was to be then expected.

Although the revolt in Barbadoes was suppressed, martial law was still in force on May 16th the same year. The Governments of the other Islands had thought it their duty to enforce that law as well, so as to frustrate any attempt at outbreak in their own precincts. The Home Government having been apprised of this insurrection, a despatch was received from Lord Bathurst—the result of an address from both Houses—to the Prince Regent, recommending the general assembly of Barbadoes to pass such remediable measures as might prove beneficial to the true interests of the Island, and thus anticipate the wish and views both of the Sovereign and the Home Government. A member present congratulated the House of Assembly on having anticipated the message, having already a measure to these ends under their consideration. Eventually the House went into committee on the proposed measure, which, with a few minor alterations, was agreed to.

In the following October, the Legislature

of Jamaica, at the recommendation of its
governor, discussed the passing of an Act
for the welfare of the slaves similar to
that adopted by the Government of Barbadoes.   The Bill was ultimately referred
to a committee for further report.   This
was made the 6th of November following,
to   the   effect   that,   agreeably   to   the
suggestions of the Government, and the
action of the Assembly in a neighbouring
island, they should proceed at once to
adopt   such   measures   as   would   be
beneficial   to   the   black   inhabitants   o
Jamaica.

The outcome of the insurrection was
most harmful to the proprietors of estates
throughout the whole of the West Indies,
most naturally those in Barbadoes, who
suffered the loss of their sugar canes by
fire, and the demolition of their sugar
machinery, as well as the destruction of
the houses on their respective estates.
We must not omit to add the great loss of
life amongst the slaves, consequent on
their resistance to the military forces.   The
owners in all respects were the greatest

sufferers, but the baneful influence of the insurrection extended to all who were in anyway interested in West Indian Possessions, either as mortgagees or owners, resident or non-resident.

Prices of estates fell. Mortgagees, who may have had properties which they deemed full margins for their advances, now found the shrinkage so great that where they had to exercise their powers the property would not realize the sum for which it stood as security. Nor were those who were fortunate enough to have their properties unencumbered much better off, many being desirous of selling, not knowing how soon another outbreak might occur; while others wished to dispose of their property and return to England or elsewhere. This they frequently found it difficult to accomplish, owing to the lack of purchasers, combined with the small comparative value received for hitherto highly-valued estates.

Mr. Coates, as well as other non-resident proprietors or mortgagees, was affected by this crisis, although he was absolved

by his father's will from all direct management of money invested in real or personal
possessions in the West Indies or elsewhere, his affairs being transacted
through the medium of trustees. These
gentlemen, however estimable, could not
foresee the course of events ; and even had
they done so it would have been difficult
to take immediate steps to guard their
trust entirely from loss.

Mr. Coates' theatrical tastes gave ample
opportunity for writers and compilers of
books and plays to exercise their pens at
his expense. Mr. Pierce Egan the elder,
the well-known author of *Tom and Jerry*,
and editor of *Life in London*, commenting
in his *Amateur Life in London* upon Mr.
Coates' acting, says :—

" Having reached their destination and
passed the night comfortably, they ('Tom'
and 'Jerry') the next morning determined
to kill an hour or so in the town by taking
a stroll arm-in-arm, when, perceiving by
a play-bill than an Amateur of Fashion
from the Theatre Royal, Drury Lane, and
Haymarket, was just come in, and would

shortly come out in a favourite character,
they immediately directed their steps
towards a barn with the hope of witnessing
a rehearsal. Chance introduced them to the
country manager, and 'Tom,' having asked
several questions about this candidate, was
assured by Mr. Mist—'Oh! he is a gentle-
man-performer, and very useful to managers, for he not only finds his own dress
and properties, but he struts and frets his
hours upon the stage without any emolu-
ments. His aversion to salary recom-
mended him to the lessee of Drury Lane,
though his services had been previously
rejected by the sub-committee.'

"'Can it be that game cock, the gay
"Lothario"?' said Tom, 'who sports an
immensity of diamonds.'

> 'Of Coates' frolics he of course well knew;
> Rare pastime for the ragamuffin crew:
> Who welcome, by the crowing of the cock,
> This hero of the buskin and the sock.'

'Oh, no,' rejoined Mr. Mist, 'that cock
don't crow now. This gentleman, I assure you, has been at a theatrical school.
He was instructed by the person who
made Master Betty a young Roscius.'

" Tom shook his head, as if he doubted the abilities of this instructed actor. To be a performer he thought as arduous a task as to be a poet, and if ' Poeta nascitur non fit,' consequently an actor must have natural abilities. 'And pray what character did this gentleman enact at Drury Lane Theatre ? '

"' Hamlet (?) Prince of Denmark,' answered Mr. Mist. ' Shakespeare is his favourite author.'

" ' And what said the critics—To be or not to be ? I suppose he repeated the character ? '

" ' Oh, sir, it was stated in the play-bill that he met with great applause, and he was announced for the character again ; but as the free list was not suspended, and our Amateur dreaded some hostility from that quarter, he performed the character by proxy, and repeated it at the little theatre in the Haymarket.'

" ' Then the gentlemen of the free list,' remarked Bob, ' are " free and easy." '

"' Yes—yes ; they laugh and cough whenever they please. Indeed, they are generally excluded whenever a full house is expected, as *ready money* is an object to the poor manager of Drury Lane Theatre. The British Press, however, is always excepted.'

" ' The British Press ? Oh ! you mean the papers,' exclaimed Tom. 'Then I daresay they were very favourable to this Amateur of Fashion ? '

" ' No, not very—indeed they don't join the managers in his puffs, notwithstanding his marked civility to them. One said he was a Methodist preacher, and sermonized the character; another assimilated him to a school-boy saying his lesson ; in short, they were very ill-natured—but, hush ! here he is. Walk in, gentlemen, and you shall hear him rehearse some of *King Richard*.'

" ' *King Richard!* What ambition ! ' thought Bob to himself. ' Late a Prince, and now a King.'

" ' I assure you,' continued Mr. Mist, ' that all his readings are new; but according to my humble observation his action does not always suit the word, for when he exclaims, " May hell make crooked my mind," he looks up to heaven.'

" ' Looks up to heaven,' exclaimed Tom. " Then this London Star makes a solecism with his eyes.'

" Our heroes now went into the barn and took a private corner, where they remained invisible. Their patience was soon exhausted, and Bob and his honourable cousin were both on the fidgets when the representative of King Richard exclaimed,—

" ' Give me a horse—'

" ' Whip !' added Tom, with stunning vociferation, before ' King Richard ' could bind up his wounds.

" The Amateur started, and betrayed consummate embarrassment, as if the horsewhip had actually made its entrance. Tom and his companion stole away and left the astonished monarch with the words, ''Twas all a dream.'

" While returning to the inn our heroes mutually commented on the ambition and folly of these Amateurs of Fashion, who not only sacrifice time and property, but

o

absolutely take abundant pains to render themselves ridiculous. 'Certainly,' said Tom, 'this *Cacoethes ludendi* has made fools of several. This infatuated youth, though not possessed of a single requisite for the stage, no doubt flatters (?) himself he is a second Kean, and, regardless of his birth and family, he will continue his strolling—

> " 'Till the broad shame comes staring in his face
> And critics hoot the blockhead as he struts.' "

Our readers will doubtless notice the inaccuracies in the foregoing. The author could scarcely have thought, that by misrepresenting the dramatic characters of Mr. Coates, he had sufficiently veiled his meaning, seeing that by his " *Gallic* " and other allusions he had openly pointed to the subject of this Memoir.

We have already recorded the marriage of Miss Tylney Long with the Hon. Wellesley Pole, and given some verses sent by Mr. Coates to Miss Long prior to that event. It is strange that those lines should have been in a manner prophetic,

for, sad to relate, this lady's husband
dissipated her fine fortune, and brought
himself and her—if we except a small
settlement—almost to penury. The
splendid demesne and mansion of
Wanstead House was brought to the
hammer to pay debts which should never
have been incurred. The sale of the
furniture and fixtures took place on June
10th, 1822 ; prior to this the property was
on view, and visited by many people from
all parts of the country. The inventory
filled a catalogue of 400 quarto pages,
published in three parts at 5s. each, and
it is said as many as 20,000 copies were
sold. This is accounted for by the
magnificence of the articles for sale,
many being unique and unrivalled. It
would be impossible to mention a tithe of
them here—comprising rare paintings,
choice old china, bronzes, sculpture,
Oriental carved ebony chairs, valuable
ivory carvings, state beds, Gobelins,
tapestries, etc., etc. The hangings of
the walls and windows of the principal
rooms were of the richest Genoa velvet,

trimmed with a triple row of gold bullion
fringe, which cost three and a half
guineas per yard. The carpets on these
apartments were embroidered in silk with
the arms of Wellesley and Long. These
two last mentioned items alone cost
60,000*l*. ten years previously, and give
some small idea of the elegance and
luxury of this princely abode. The sale
lasted a month, and although some few
articles fetched good prices (the plate
realizing 15*s*. per oz.) the result was
ultimately a terrible loss to the owners on
the first cost. Upwards of 20,000*l*. was
received during the first six days before
a quarter of the catalogue was reached;
but this did not go far to satisfy or stay
the deluge of debt; as after all fittings
and furniture were sold, the noble pile
itself was razed to the ground and the
materials disposed of in lots. Even this
expedient, together with the sale of other
old and valuable estates, did not satisfy
the Moloch of debt. The ruined debtor
then had recourse to France in order to
escape the then penalties of insolvency,

and there he might have remained for
years had not some intercession been
made on his behalf by his friends and
family, whereby he was appointed, by
announcement in the *London Gazette* of
Tuesday, August 6th, 1822, one of his
Majesty's attendants; the real position
being stated as "Gentleman usher, daily
waiter to his Majesty." The most im-
portant benefit to the holder of this
position was the freedom from arrest
which his Majesty's attendants then enjoyed; so was this scheme contrived to
enable a ruined gentleman to return to
his native land.

The papers, true to their original course,
could not let Mr. Coates alone, no matter
how various his pursuits. After almost
giving up appearing in theatrical characters, in the year 1823, he took great
interest in the Rev. George Irving, of
Presbyterian notoriety, whom the *John
Bull* newspaper—then a most satirical
journal, not the sober and staid publication of the present day—lost no opportunity of deriding, together with his

supporters. It may interest some of our readers to see a specimen of the articles that a paper—then, as now, presumably devoted to the acting members of the State religion—at that time published; so we here give verbatim a few extracts on this subject, and epitomize those that are too long. Even a physical defect of the reverend gentleman was made a subject for ridicule.

John Bull, p. 237, July, 1823.—" Dr. Squintum (Rev. G. Irving): 'Crow a little, if you please, Mr. Romeo. Don't waste precious moments; come in and be saved, or stay out and be d—d' (Pew-opener's exordium). After which may be sung a new ballad, entitled 'Dr. Squintum,' to the tune of 'Nancy Dawson':—

.   .   .   .   .

'Let Squintum Zanies go in pairs
As other humbugs do at fairs,
And *Montague* upon the stairs
Harangues with "Cockadoodle."'

"'Walk up, ladies and gentlemen, if you please; walk in and see the wonderful Dr. Squintum, just arrived from Glasgow. The most magnificent preacher as ever

was seen in the world, or anywhere else.
Tumble up, ladies ; mind your pockets.
Now, Mr. Basillico, tip the gentlefolks
a speech ; here they come. Stand out of
the way, you poor-looking chap, we want
no paupers here. Now's your time, just
going to begin. . . .' "

This tirade is followed up the following
week, August 3rd, 1823, by another,
equally inimical :—

" Dr. Squintum.—The public are beginning to open their eyes to the Presbyterian
quackery with which at first they were
so surprisingly taken. The most zealous
of Squintum's adherents and followers are
repenting them of the rashness with which
they committed themselves by an avowal
of their admiration. He falls off, however,
from that tipsy popularity which for a
week or two he acquired. It therefore
becomes necessary for his brother quacks
to keep up the humbug, by which de-
fection from the Established Church is to
be promoted, and rant and cant exalted
above reason and religion. . . ."

The article then goes on to note what

the Rev. John Clayton, Jun., of the Poultry Chapel, said in reference to the Rev. George Irving, eulogizing him and comparing him to a young eagle out of the north, who has lately escaped from his nest. The writer in *John Bull* proceeds to criticize the above descriptive account, asking, " Why is Mr. Irving like an eagle, and at present, says Mr. John Clayton, dwells chiefly amongst rocks and caverns ? If he be any bird at all, he is a crowing cock upon his own dung-hill, fed and attended by Mr. *Romeo Coates,* whose affection for that bird has led him to devote himself particularly to his service."

Surely the foregoing are some of the most curious critiques ever printed upon a popular preacher, whose chief fault, according to this religious paper, was his being a Dissenter—if that difference of opinion can be construed as an error. We may also infer that it was all the same to most of, if not all, the papers about that period, whether Mr. Coates appeared as an Amateur on the public stage for and on behalf of a private or public charity, or accorded his aid and support in a totally opposite direction as just mentioned. No credit was to be given him by these captious critics for the one or the other. They had decreed that he should be written down, and written down he generally was by all. To those who pinned their faith to news-paper reports and critiques it might have been difficult to arrive at any second judg-ment; but at the present distance from the date of the occurrence of the events related we can view them in a more im-partial spirit, and we shall presently have to record the opinions of persons of a position in society equal to that of Mr. Coates, and also those of his superiors, which outweigh, as we think, those of his detractors.

An interesting, humorous and satirical work appeared during 1825, written in verse, and entitled " The English Spy." The writer, who faithfully chronicles characters of that period, is bound to mention Mr. Coates. The reference appears on page 206 :—

. . . .

"And see ! where everybody notes
The Star of Fashion, 'Romeo' Coates
The Amateur appears.
But where ? ah ! where, say shall I tell,
Are the brass cocks and cockle-shell ?
I'll hazard *rouge et noir*.
If it but speak, can tales relate
Of many an equipage's fate,
And may of many more."

(Note appended.)—" Poor 'Romeo's' brilliancy is somewhat dulled, and though not quite a fallen star he must not run on *black* too long lest his diamond-hilted sword should be the price of his folly."

The foregoing note seems to imply that Mr. Coates was addicted to the board of green cloth, in other words a gamester; but this was not the case. We do not, however, mean to assert that he did not play occasionally. We must seek other causes than this for his equipages being put down, in the large sums he had lent (most of which were never repaid), and his lavish expenditure during his residence in England; and besides, the depreciatory influence of the war and revolt had caused a decline in West Indian values, which was destined to become more serious at a later period.

MRS. COATES.

Page 203.

CHAPTER X.

Mr. Coates' marriage with Miss Robinson at St. George's, Hanover Square—Issue of this union—Canons and Wanstead House—Death of the Honourable Mrs. Wellesley Pole—Troubles still continuing in the West Indies, causing loss to the holders of estates and securities in these islands—Mr. Coates retires to Boulogne, where he lives several years, principally at the Hôtel du Nord—His meeting there with King Louis Philippe.

ON the 6th day of September, 1823, Mr. Coates was married [1] at St. George's, Hanover Square, by special licence, to Miss Emma Anne Robinson, daughter of Lieutenant William McDowell Robinson, of his Majesty's Navy, whose family for the previous two centuries had been, and are still, officers in that illustrious service. The lady, one of a large family, was born early in the present century at Chigwell in Essex, where her younger days were passed, and was sister to the late Commander Edward Robinson, R.N., of *Amelia*

---

[1] Copy of certificate in authors' possession.

notoriety,[2] and the late Vice-Admiral Charles Gepp Robinson, who had the honour of attending upon her Majesty in one or two of her visits to the Highlands. The Queen courteously alludes to him in her book entitled " Leaves from the Journal of Our Life in the Highlands," vol. i. pp. 271-272.[3] Mr. Coates met the lady of his choice at a friend's house, and, lest our statements might be supposed to be too partial, we take this opportunity of making a few extracts from the *Lady's Magazine* for August, 1830; which has a fine steel portrait of Mrs. Coates as " the wife of the celebrated Amateur of Fashion." The article commences by saying that— " Every man has his foibles and faults, so had Amateur Coates; but malevolence might attack ninety-nine out of every hundred with as much justice as there was in the outcry against the eccentric gentleman; who, whatever may be said of his weaknesses, erred always on the side of benevolence, and committed his very

[2] See O'Byrne's " Naval Biography," 1849.
[3] For details of this officer's career, see O'Byrne's " Naval Biography."

greatest follies in her service. We have seen him play 'Romeo' for the benefit of public and private charities repeatedly, and we have .afterwards seen every point of his acting misrepresented. Were we determined to carp at all the varieties and follies of the great, we might indeed be well employed. What was there more in the 'Romeo' of Mr. Coates than in the 'Queen Elizabeth' of the Marchioness of Londonderry, who, for her vanity in assuming the sovereignty, was beheaded by a monthly magazine, and had the mortification to see her headless portrait published to some two or three hundred readers in a seven-shilling book! What is there more in Mr. Coates dying a second time as 'Romeo' (supposing such to have been the case) than there is in the said Marchioness offering to pay all the expenses of another plate if the said magazine would but allow her to appear a second time, but with the advantage of her head on, instead of as before, in imitation of the sign of *A good woman*?"

The papers, faithful to their occupation

of misrepresenting everything connected with Mr. Coates, stated that " he appeared at the altar in his dress sword, and that immediately after the ceremony the happy pair set off for Portsmouth." Both of these assertions were equally false. He wore no sword at all; and the happy pair went immediately to Henley-on-Thames.

Mr. Coates had so long retired from those scenes in which he attained singular notoriety that we should hardly have cared to disturb his seclusion but for the pleasure of doing justice to his heart and to his taste. The goodness of the former may be testified by many charitable institutions; the elegance of the latter is, we think, abundantly exhibited in the portrait which embellishes this work.

The issue of the auspicious union was two children; the eldest a boy, who died in his youth, the other scarce survived the days of infancy.

Mr. Coates now simply played the *rôle* of an independent private gentleman, much met with in society, at the theatres, and at those town and country resorts then visited by the fashionable world. He was partial to an occasional run across the Channel; but his voice was heard no more upon the public stage, although he would frequently gratify a host and hostess, as well as his own guests, with recitations and some-times with private theatricals. No induce-ment could make him at this time appear at a theatre for the benefit of any actor or actress, although he was seldom appealed to in vain if requested to aid them with money. It must not be thought, however, that this gentleman's absence from scenes where he had been so well known was the end of his popularity, for to the time of his death he was an object of interest to the curious, and known by many towards his latter days more by repute than by ocular demonstration.

To recur to Wanstead House; it is strange that this palatial abode—to-gether with its prototype Canons, the magnificent residence of the first Duke of Chandos—the owner of which was related to the Duke through Cassandra, the latter's second wife, was rebuilt about the time Canons was begun. These noblemen seemed to vie with each other in magnificence, each employing different architects, painters, etc., and during the three decades of the last century it was a matter of dispute which mansion excelled the other in splendour, though doubtless the palm should have been and ultimately was awarded to Canons. As a further instance of the curious connection between these two houses, we record the following fact.

Upon the dismantling and pulling down of Canons in 1747, the greater portion of the noble columns were sold to the then owner of Wanstead House, who formed a portico to the mansion with them; this in its turn was demolished with the house, as we have seen, seventy years later.

On the 12th of September, 1825, died the once worshipped Mrs. Wellesley Pole, *née* Miss Tylney Long. This lady, born to inherit wealth and station that could command every luxury and desire, had lost all the large possessions of her family by the prodigality and recklessness of her husband; and the agony of that loss was increased by the conduct of one who might at least have shown some remorse for the wreck he had made of a noble fortune. It is said that the sale of her ancestral home with all its costly belongings preyed so much on this lady's constitution—already shattered by domestic anxieties and grief—that it hastened her death. Many of the leading papers of the day had long articles upon this unfortunate woman's troubles. A short extract from one will show the general feeling for her, and the respect in which she was held :—

The Age—leading article, September 18th, 1825.—"At the period of her unfortunate marriage, Mrs. Pole might be considered the most singularly favoured lady of the day, for in addition to a pleasing person, engaging manners, and more than ordinary accomplishments, she possessed a larger fortune probably than any commoner in the kingdom; and thus highly gifted, she blazed in the world a

P

prize that princes well might and even did envy. There was no rank that could be compromised, no talents that could be sacrificed, and no fortune that could be disadvantageously disposed in a union with her; and the man who, contending against the importunities of one of the blood Royal, the addresses of many of our gentry, could attract and eventually triumph over the affections of this heiress, might well be considered at once the most singularly fortunate man of his time. The fortune Mrs. Pole bestowed with her hand upon the object of her choice was nearly 60,000*l.* per annum, with the mansion of her family at Wanstead, considered the most splendid place in the kingdom; and with neither the addition of property or the want of it, her only desideratum in a matrimonial connection was the responsive affection of him she married, and the endearment of domestic ties. To her no luxury could be a novelty, no society an elevation, for her halls had sheltered the princes of other lands, and feasted those of her own country in prosperity. She stood, therefore, high in the world, an enviable and an envied woman. There was no home that could be made too delightful for her, no earthly happiness to which she was not entitled; she was courted by the affluent, idolized by the poor, and walked upright in the sight of her Maker. By a marriage which should have realized all these just expectations, she became the very reverse of all her own heart could fancy or hope, or the world could possibly believe. In a few years she was forsaken, when she ought to have been cherished or rather worshipped, her almost Eastern income squandered away, the gorgeous mansion of her father razed to the ground, herself and children reduced to subsist on a reserved pittance in humble privacy, and even that privacy rudely broken in upon, and her gentle spirit at length released from all worldly suffering, leaving no other legacy to her wretched offspring than their mother's broken heart."

Such, then, was the sad end of one of the most favoured women of the century,

who was so fortunately situated as regarded
wealth and position as to be able to have
given any ordinary man every thing he
could wish for, but whose vast estate
could not eventually satisfy debts which
had no right to be contracted, let alone
paid from her fortune. As we have seen,
her fortune was ultimately swallowed up
by one who should have done his utmost
to have kept and improved it. Unfortunately this much-lamented lady was
not, nor will be, the only one who
made a great error in the object of her
choice, and possibly had she been able to
foresee its dire consequences, she would
have halted even on the threshold of the
church before linking herself to such a
being.

Mr. Coates' lines to this lady—given in
an earlier chapter—hint that many worshipped her for her wealth alone. The
unfortunate sequel proves this to have
been too true.

The troubles in the West Indian Islands
were prominent during the early part of
the third decade of the present century.

Although no serious outbreak was presented, yet the tone of the negro inhabitants of these islands was defiant and irritable : this, connected with other circumstances, paved the way for the abolition measures adopted a few years later. During the years 1824 and 1825 several meetings were held in London by West Indian proprietors, merchants, and others, who had previously formed themselves into an influential committee to protect their rights. Nevertheless, the outlook was not satisfactory to those whose incomes were in a great measure derived from possessions, trade, or investments in this Archipelago, and the falling-off in the value of these properties had made itself felt in 1816. From this period the slow but steady decadence of those beautiful islands may be traced. Mr. Coates, with others, felt these effects, and it was not until some years later, viz. the time of the grant of 20,000,000*l.* for the freeing of the slaves, that the holders and others interested in West Indian property could be said to be relieved from anxiety. Even

this large sum, disbursed for so laudable a purpose, did not prove a panacea
for all their troubles, as the present value
and trade of these islands testify. Surely
much remains to be done for them, either
by promoting colonization, or by growing
commodities which will compete favourably with those of other countries. Mr.
Coates' pecuniary position was affected,
but perhaps not so much as that of
other proprietors. However, early in the
Thirties, through temporary monetary
pressure he retired to Boulogne, as
many persons similarly situated had done
before. No doubt this necessity might
have been obviated had he wisely entered
an appearance, or come to some arrangement about several actions pending
against him. As prudence or foresight
had not dictated this course, he was forced
to make an exile of himself for a time as
the price of his neglect. Possibly Mr.
Coates may have had more poignant
reasons than we have been able to trace
for his conduct in this matter: at any
rate he was better off than nine-tenths of

those who made Boulogne-sur-Mer a refuge in those days ; for he was able to engage the best suite of rooms in the Hôtel du Nord, the best in the little town. During his sojourn at Boulogne he was an object of almost as much interest as he had been in London, and was much sought after by the English colony. Mr. Coates remained at Boulogne for several years, making various trips to Paris and other places of interest on the Continent, and living as a private gentleman. It was not until the year 1840 that an incident occurred to bring his name again prominently before the public. In that year King Louis Philippe visited Boulogne, for the purpose of thanking the inhabitants of the town for their loyal conduct on the occasion of the landing of Prince Louis Napoleon, in August. This attempt had caused the relations between England and France to become somewhat strained. The event was aggravated, so the French thought, by the fact that the vessel, the captain, and most of the crew chartered by the Bonapartists were English, and the English residents resolved to present an address to the King of the French, assuring him of their sympathy and loyalty; and with that purpose a meeting was held on the 21st of August, 1840, to decide on the terms of the address. This was, no doubt, the outcome of King Louis Philippe's reply to Mr. Coates a day or so previously, an account of which was given by all the London papers. Insignificant as the circumstance may appear, it had a great effect upon both French and English opinion, and aided in a measure to allay the irritable feeling that prevailed among the residents of both countries. The *Morning Chronicle* of August 21st, 1840, gives the best report of this incident that we have been able to find, in the following paragraphs :—

" Their Majesties, almost immediately after their arrival, proceeded to the Theatre, where they were extremely well received, but it would be incorrect to say that their presence at any time during their stay excited any feeling approaching to enthusiasm. On their return from the

Theatre a circumstance occurred which will, I suppose, interest you in England, as it has caused a very great and highly-gratifying sensation here. It seems, indeed, to give more pleasure to the French than to the English. Mr. Coates, an English gentleman of fortune, permanently occupies the best suite of apartments in the Hôtel du Nord, the only hotel where persons of very high rank can be fitly accommodated. With the national feeling of a well-bred gentleman, Mr. Coates, immediately upon the Queen's arrival, surrendered his apartments to her Majesty's convenience. Last night as the Royal pair were ascending the stairs of the Hotel they encountered Mr. Coates, and the King very graciously thanked him for his politeness. Mr. Coates, who is an enthusiastic old gentleman, answered by shouting in French, 'Long live the King and Queen; prosperity to France and England, and eternal peace between them!' The sentiments were repeated by the many persons in attendance, and after all others were silent, the King himself exclaimed in a loud voice, as if to enhance the compliment in the English language, 'Prosperity to England and to France, eternal peace between them; and while I live there shall be!' His Majesty afterwards translated his words into French, and they were heartily responded to by his suite. As I said, this circumstance has produced a wonderful impression here, and one that has unquestionably served his Majesty with the Boulonnais. . . . "

With the foregoing account of Mr. Coates' efforts in the praiseworthy attempt to conciliate the French, we bring this chapter to a close.

CHAPTER XI.

Mr. Coates returns to England, having first made satisfactory conditions—His first London residence at
this period—His objection to being publicly
called " Romeo " Coates—Anecdote of Mr. Coates
and a French Minister at a dinner party—Bolton
House, Sir Thomas Noon Talfourd's residence:
Mr. Coates a frequent visitor—Lord Campbell's
and others' opinions on Mr. Coates' dramatic
readings and acting.

SHORTLY after his meeting with King
Louis Philippe, Mr. Coates, like many
other self-banished persons, ardently
desired to return to London, the scene
of his former dramatic efforts and diamond and curricle notoriety. But how
to accomplish this was the question,
knowing, as he did, that by his non-
appearance to an action brought against
him judgment had gone by default—a
more unpleasant circumstance in the
times of which we are writing than at
present. There were other large claims

unsatisfied besides the case just named. At last, satisfactory conditions were made between Mr. Coates and his largest creditors—not that a composition was offered or made, the arrangement agreed upon savoured more of the *post obit* kind, as the debts, together with interest, were to be paid on Mr. Coates' decease, from funds he had an appointment over but could not touch. This difficulty being removed, we find Mr. Coates residing in Connaught Square, Hyde Park, in the early part of 1843 ; from thence he removed to 13, Portman Street, Portman Square, and ultimately to a more commodious residence, 28, Montague Square, W. After Mr. Coates' return to the metropolis he naturally resorted to his former places of amusement and walks. During one of his peregrinations, familiar association led him to saunter up St. James's Street. In passing either Arthur's or Brooks' Club, the well-known figure— wearing well-creased Hessian boots, a bygone fashion of at least three decades to which he still adhered—attracted the attention of a gentleman who was sitting at an open window. This person said to some friends in the back of the room, " Well, to be sure, here's 'Romeo' Coates!" The response was an immediate rush to the window to see the subject of this gentleman's exclamation. Mr. Coates' stride took him a few paces past, but having heard his well-worn stage name mentioned, he turned round, came to the window from which the voice proceeded, stood in front of, and with great politeness raised his hat and said, "My name, gentlemen, is Robert Coates." Then bowing again, he resumed his hat and walk with a calm and dignified air.

An anecdote is told of how Mr. Coates most unwillingly gave offence at a dinner to a French Minister of State. The Amateur had been asked, after the removal of the cloth, to oblige the guests with a reading of Fitzgerald's " Ode on the Death of Nelson," the gentleman expressing this wish having heard the ode read by Mr. Coates upon a previous occasion at Sir Thomas Noon Talfourd's. Mr. Coates immediately complied with the request, and not until the last stanza was reached did it flash across the mind of the host that a well-known and respected member of the French nation was present. The Minister, however, showed good taste by waiting till Mr. Coates had finished his recitation, when he rose and said that he, as a Frenchman, had never before had his feelings so much hurt in English society.

Of course the host immediately assured him that he was confident the gentleman who requested the reading of the ode was actuated by the best motives, and would not have done so had he thought for one moment that he would wound the feelings of a fellow-guest. These sentiments were re-echoed by the innocent cause of this little unpleasantness, who reminded the Minister that, although by birth a Frenchman, his Excellency was an Irishman by extraction, like the author of the ode, and added that he hoped he would look upon himself as a member of the Irish nation, at least for that evening.

He then proceeded to say, that as the Minister had alluded to his Royal Master, he would add : "There is no gentleman present who has received more kindness and attention at the hands of the French King than he, Mr. Coates, had." He was here alluding to the Boulogne incident mentioned in the last chapter, which was said to have raised the funds 4 per cent. " During the few succeeding days he volunteered, if necessary, to go to Paris and solicit an interview with Louis Philippe, who, as an illustrious refugee, had resided for some time during 1805 at Twickenham, and, he believed, knew the author of the ode he had just read. He felt sure that Louis Philippe would not, as the exiled Duc d'Orleans, have objected to the destruction of Napoleon's fleet by the gallant Nelson." This argument, so forcibly put, had a soothing effect upon the injured Minister's mind; he good-naturedly waived his resentment, and joined with the assembled guests in making the evening pass harmoniously.

At this time, Mr. Coates was a frequent

visitor and guest at Bolton House, the residence of Sir Thomas Noon Talfourd, where he frequently gave recitations and took part in private theatricals.

Bolton House was a well-known resort of men of letters, actors and others devoted to the arts and sciences ; and anyone who there ventured upon a display of rhetorical or dramatic powers was sure of a critical if not appreciative audience. Among those to be found at this hospitable mansion were the owner's fellow judges, together with some well-known members of the bar ; gentlemen as well qualified, perhaps, to pass an opinion as the professed critics of to-day. We may therefore inquire what opinion was entertained, by such a variously-composed company, of Mr. Coates' achievements ; and we find that they failed to understand why the acting of this gentleman in his former days had been so greatly censured ; also, that many who came with prejudiced minds became his most enthusiastic admirers upon witnessing his acting or hearing his recitation. One of his most laudatory hearers was the

late Lord Justice Campbell, who with his
scholarly and kindly-hearted host joined
with others in recording their approbation
of Mr. Coates. Such opinions as these
are worthy of respect; especially when we
take into consideration Sir Thomas Noon
Talfourd's excellence as a dramatic writer,
his tragedy of *Ion* alone entitling him to be
placed in the first rank of such authors.
Nor were his prose writings much below
the standard of his great play; his
" Memorials of Charles Lamb" are acknowledged by many to be the best authority
on that immortal humorist. Many articles in the *Edinburgh Review*, and the
New Monthly Magazine testify to the
literary skill of this generous and noble-
minded judge, whose labours, while he
sat in Parliament for his native town of
Reading, should ever be remembered by
the writers and authors of this kingdom;
but it is to be feared that few of those who
have reaped and are still reaping the
benefits of his exertions, know that to him
they are indebted for the Copyright Act of
1842. The death of this highly-cultured,

simple-hearted, modest and upright judge and man was truly lamentable. It occurred upon the 13th of March, 1854, while he was in the act of charging the Grand Jury at Stafford. He had just expressed his regret at the gulf that existed between the various classes of society in this country— partly, he felt, through ignorance and an imperfect understanding—when he fell forward and expired. Thus died one of the most liberal-minded and kind-hearted men that ever sat on the judicial bench, one whose judgments were always tempered with mercy.

CHAPTER XII.

ONE of Mr. Coates' oldest friends used
to say that he had seldom met a man more
quick at repartee, or who could give a
Roland for an Oliver with greater spirit.
His wit and readiness in retaliation frequently stood him in good stead, as the
following will prove. One day, while
dining with a party of savants at Richmond, a well-known wit and fellow-guest
thought to add to his laurels by humorous
allusions to Mr. Coates, and especially
to his theatrical days. To do this more
pointedly he was at last bound to ask Mr.
Coates a question; and he replied that
he could answer at once if the questioner

would assure him that his reason for seeking the information was not to exhibit his wit at his (Mr. Coates') expense. This courteous reply had the desired effect; the great satirist remained as quiet as possible during the rest of the evening.

We now pass to a more serious subject, which, although beginning in gaiety, ended in death. On February 15th, 1848, Mr. Coates attended Allcroft's grand annual concert at Drury Lane, and passed a very enjoyable evening; but no sooner had he seated himself in his carriage to return home, than he recollected having left his opera-glass—the gift of an old friend deceased—in the box. He sprang out of the carriage, and, in making his way across Russell Street (then much crowded), he was knocked down and run over by a hansom cab, alleged to have been carelessly and furiously driven. The driver, so soon as he saw what had happened, increased his speed and made off. A crowd having assembled around the unfortunate gentleman, Mr. Coates was at once removed to King's College Hospital, where the house surgeon, Mr. Alfred Barton, showed him every skill and attention. He discovered that his patient had several ribs broken, as well as a laceration of the breast, together with several bruises upon his legs and other parts of his body, caused by his having been trodden on. In spite of these severe injuries, coupled with his advanced age (75), hopes were entertained of his recovery; and he was ultimately removed to his residence in Montague Square. Here he was attended by Sir Benjamin Brodie, Dr. Webster, Mr. Tatum, and William Bernard Robinson, M.R.C.S., who were one and all unremitting in their attention; but in spite of all their united skill, erysipelas set in on the Sunday following, which next day, unfortunately, ended fatally.

The day after (Tuesday) Mr. Wakley, M.P., held an inquest upon the body of the deceased. After a close inquiry, the jury found that Mr. Coates had met his death through being knocked down and run over by a hansom cab, the driver of which they considered had been guilty of gross negligence; but this person not having been found, they were obliged to return a verdict of manslaughter against some person unknown; and that the police be instructed to make every inquiry with a view of bringing the person to justice. The inspector present on behalf of the police stated they had already done so, but would continue their investigations; at present they only knew it was one of Hansom's patent cabs drawn by a grey horse.

Mr. Coates was interred a few days after at Kensal Green Cemetery; and was followed to his last resting-place by a large body of friends, who, one and all, deeply lamented his tragic end.

The papers and periodicals of that time announced the above facts with more or less regret. The leading journal of the time stated that the deceased gentleman had for some years retired from public life, and was much respected for his charitable disposition. This organ had, in the days of Mr. Coates' histrionic efforts, published some very severe criticisms upon his acting, so that its respectful mention came with greater force from a former severe critic.

As so many have borne tribute to Mr. Coates' character both before and after his sad death, we will content ourselves with two or three examples, and shall first mention that of the late Lord William Pitt Lennox. At the zenith of Mr. Coates' notoriety, Lord William Lennox was a youth at Westminster School, and well remembered the curricle and white horses driven by Mr. Coates in the Park, as well as some of his theatrical displays. Lord William speaks of the histrionic powers of Mr. Coates as those of " an *amateur*, possessed of a good private fortune and a devotion to the stage, coupled with a liberal education and a gentlemanlike character and bearing, the very antipodes to many who attempted to pose after him as Amateurs of Fashion."

The writer of an article on Mr. Coates' Thespian career in the *New Monthly Magazine* for 1827, concludes by saying : " He was ever described as a good-natured man, not at all deficient in sense, and who now sustains in private life a most respectable character."

An old beau who gave his reminiscences to the public at the beginning of the present reign (but who would not publish his name) mentions Mr. Coates as "not being one bit like Pea-green H. (Haynes) and others, who made away with all they had while keeping a dashing equipage, but one who, while obtaining notoriety, contented himself with apartments in Craven Street as a bachelor." For this many blamed him, and, perhaps, had he removed from those apartments shortly after his public appearance on the London stage for the first time he would have saved himself the unpleasantness caused by his landlady's conduct in the matter we have related.

We regret that it will be our duty to record in the following chapter the controversy caused by the inadvertence of a well-known chronicler, whose attack upon the subject of this Memoir was afterwards refuted by relatives who were then alive.

CHAPTER XIII.

Mrs. Coates did not long continue a widow,
She married, on the 23rd of the December
following, an old friend and associate of
her late husband, Mark Boyd, Esq., second
son of Edward Boyd, Esq., J.P., of Merton
House, Wigton, N.B., and brother to the
once well-known Benjamin Boyd of Australia and New Zealand fame, whose death
has never been satisfactorily accounted
for. With this gentleman she resided in
various parts of the town and country,
until, finding household management too
troublesome, she finally settled down at

the Oatlands Park Hotel, Weybridge, in a charming neighbourhood, and one much favoured by her first husband, Mr. Coates.

From 1848 to 1868 only occasional mention was made in the various periodicals of the celebrated " Amateur of Fashion," until Walter Thornbury made one of the most calumnious attacks ever published upon Mr. Coates in the *Belgravia Magazine* for January, 1868. This, although it contains much that the reader has seen in these pages, we find it necessary to give in detail :—

" About 1801,[1] one of the most conspicuous characters in the Park was a tall, thin West Indian planter,[2] with a sallow, wrinkled (?) skin, dressed in costly furs, who paraded the drives in a shell-shaped

---

[1] This date is entirely wrong, Mr. Coates was not in England for the second time until after his father's death—in fact, somewhere near the beginning of 1809 ; and it was not until 1811 that Mr. Coates started his noted curricle.—AUTHORS.

[2] Mr. Coates, in 1801, would have been about twenty-eight years of age, and thirty-six when he arrived in 1809.—AUTHORS.

carriage drawn by two fine white horses. The eccentric but handsome vehicle was covered by the owner's heraldic device—a cock crowing. This shallow, inane but cunning-looking man was the celebrated tragedian, Mr. 'Romeo' Coates. He was supposed incorrectly to be a second Crœsus, and he appeared at London balls covered with as many diamonds as Count Esterhazy, who was popularly supposed to drop 3000l. pounds worth of them every night he went out; his buttons, even his knee buckles, glistened with diamonds. Inanely vain and utterly foolish, 'Romeo' Coates appeared on the stage as Shakespeare's youthful lover, first at Bath and then at the Haymarket. The ridiculous being wore a spangled cloak of sky-blue silk, red pantaloons much too tight, a white muster vest, an enormous bolster cravat, a Charles II. wig, and an opera hat.[3] No burlesque was ever half so funny; he bowed to the audience in the most

---

[3] Mr. Coates' usual dress has been previously described.—AUTHORS.

extravagant way; with a hideous grin he took snuff in the middle of the balcony-scene; and on some one asking him for a pinch handed round his box to the nearest spectators. He dragged 'Juliet' from the tomb like a sack of potatoes; when finally he had to die, he put down his opera-hat for a pillow, and swept a place clean with a dirty silk handkerchief. Three times (?) did this extraordinary idiot die for the amusement of the house. This half fool, half cheat was at last driven from the stage for pocketing money he had obtained under pretence of playing for a charitable object. He retired to Boulogne and there married some foolish woman who had been duped by his pre-tended wealth." [4]

The above article called forth the following letters from those best entitled to protest; namely, some of Mr. Coates' associates and relatives who were then alive:—

---

[4] We need not remind the reader that the latter assertion is as incorrect as almost all of the fore-going.—AUTHORS.

From the *Standard*, Jan. 20th, 1868:—

" THE LATE MR. ' ROMEO ' COATES.

" *To the Editor.*

" SIR,—With your invincible sense of justice as regards statements made in your widely-circulated journal when affecting the feelings of others, I am persuaded you will allow me to contradict with warrantable indignation a most unjust and unfounded aspersion on the character of the late Mr. Coates, which forms the subject of a notice in your morning and evening impression of the 14th inst., copied from *Belgravia*, from which I make the following extract : ' This half fool, half cheat was at last driven from the stage for pocketing money he had obtained under pretence of playing for a charitable object.' To this, no other reply is due than that it is a base and calumnious falsehood. I have passed over as unworthy of notice the further remarks which represent the character of the late Mr. Coates, as there are many persons still alive who can testify to his excellent qualities and high bearing as a GENTLEMAN; and also he was well known as such to a large number of friends in an elevated social position who have passed to their rest. But as a set-off to the writer in *Belgravia* of 1868, whose paragraph before mentioned has greatly increased in its importance by its publication in your paper, allow me to lay before you the annexed short extracts from the *Times* of the 24th February, 1848, in referring to Mr. Coates' death, and also to a previous one on Mr. Coates in the *Lady's Magazine* of July, 1830, a time much nearer to the facts to which *Belgravia* alludes, and consequently nearer to the truth.

> " I remain, sir,
> " Your obedient servant,
> " VERITAS.

" From the *Times*, February 24th, 1848:—

" ' The deceased gentleman had long since retired into private life, and was held in universal esteem for his charitable character.' "

(Here follows a portion of the article we have already given from the *Lady's Magazine,* July, 1830.)

" To the Editor of the Standard.

"Sir,—I have read with the deepest pain and surprise in your impression of the 14th inst. an extract copied from the *Belgravia* in reference to the late Mr. Robert Coates, who, some fifty years since, was familiarly known as ' Romeo' Coates. I do not enter into any of my late friend's eccentricities, either in respect to his curricle of unique build (which I never saw,—but I may here mention that a London journal now before me of the 24th February, 1848, describes it as one of the very neatest things to be seen in London before or since) or to his histrionic powers, not having witnessed them in any London or Bath theatre. But this much I know, that they were always given to promote the good cause of charity, Mr. Coates being invariably a liberal contributor himself, sometimes 100*l*. or 50*l*., as the case might be. I have, however, seen him join in private theatricals at the house of his hospitable and cherished friend Judge Talfourd, and I recollect that those who came to laugh remained to praise ; for his recitations from Shakespeare were so good that the author of *Ion* expressed to the writer of this letter his astonishment at the ability he displayed, in which he was heartily joined by the late Lord Campbell and other distinguished occupants of the bench and bar then present. In fact, the visitors at Bolton House could not understand why their forefathers were so fastidious in finding fault with the amateur acting of ' Romeo ' Coates of former days. But the point in regard to the concluding paragraph from the *Belgravia*, in which the honesty and integrity of my late amiable friend are so cruelly and unjustly belied, Mr. Coates *never* in his life had a money transaction connected with a theatre. He was a frequent contributor in purse, but never a receiver. No man was more deserving of the tribute paid his memory by the *Times*.[5]

" As I am myself prepared, also two of the deceased gentleman's nearest relatives, —one an admiral in British service, the other an author like yourself,—to give the most unqualified denial to the falsehood imposed in the *Belgravia* and copied by your journal, I ask you, in common justice to the memory of the late Mr. Coates, to insert this letter in your earliest impression ; for in the opinion of those we have consulted a more unjustifiable libel was never published.   I enclose my card,

" And have the honour to remain, sir,

" Your obedient servant,

" A Friend of the late Mr. Robert Coates for more than a quarter of a century.

" January 17th, 1868.

" P.S.—I regret the length at which I am compelled to address you, but in

---

[5] February 24th, 1848, before quoted.

vindicating the character of one whom I greatly esteemed against his black and envenomed assailant in the *Belgravia,* I must take leave to mention a fact unknown to his family till the tomb had closed upon him. While a gay bachelor in London, during the prosperous times for West Indian proprietors, he had disbursed in private charity, and principally amongst the *dependent families of those who strut and fret their hour upon the stage, not less than between* 4000*l. and* 5000*l.* This only confirmed the impression made in the mind of the writer—that Mr. Coates was a man that did good by stealth and 'blushed to find it fame.' If he was somewhat ostentatious as a young man of his curricle and horses (especially the latter) it was innocent; for often he has told me what the Duke of York once said to him : ' Why, Coates, the Regent and you drive the best horses in London ! ' "

From the *Standard,* Jan. 23rd, 1868 :—

" ' Romeo ' Coates.

" Sir,—Will you allow me to supply an

omission in my letter of the 17th inst. ?
Mr. Coates was married at St. George's,
Hanover Square, *not in France*, to the
daughter of a naval officer, universally
esteemed, the friend throughout a long
life—as he had been the companion on
the quarter-deck—of Admiral Sir Elias
Harvey, Sir Edmund Owen, the Hon.
Frederick Paul Irby, etc., etc. ; and left, in
addition to other children, two sons following out the same honourable career in that
gallant profession in which from father
to son his family had gained distinction
and honour for a period of two centuries.
One of these sons is now an admiral ; the
other (who recently died) was a captain
in the navy, and saw much active service
during the last war, being severely
wounded in that hard-fought frigate
action, which, in regard to casualties,
excelled, I believe, those on board the
Shannon in her engagement with the
Chesapeake—I allude to the action
fought by Honourable Paul Irby in the
Amelia with a French frigate *L'Arethusa*. The *Amelia* had 145 killed and

wounded out of 300; *L'Arethusa* even more.

"I have the honour to be, sir,

"Your most obedient servant,

"A FRIEND of the late Mr. Robert Coates for upwards of a quarter of a century."

The foregoing letters brought the following apologetic reply from Mr. Walter Thornbury, which we shall further remark upon.

From the *Standard*, Jan. 24th, 1868:—

"*To the Editor.*

"SIR,—Your two correspondents have emptied their little bottles of vitriol over me with a most superfluous anger. My father had repeatedly met Mr. 'Romeo' Coates in society, and he also saw him on the stage. It was from him I chiefly drew my sketch of 'Romeo' Coates' personal appearance and manner. It was, however, to one of Captain Gronow's pleasant volumes that I was indebted for the obnoxious paragraph which has excited such indignation. I have hitherto found the patriarchical dandy a most reliable reporter of old gossip. I can only express my *sincere regret* at having disseminated a scandal *which appears to be unjust*, and to express my pleasure that the *detracting story* is *untrue*. It is one of the serious penalties awaiting any author who writes about the times of the Regency that he never can be certain that what he is saying may not give pain to some survivor of that lamentable epoch.

"I remain, sir,
"Your most obedient servant,
"Walter Thornbury.

"Fonthill Cottage, Dorking,
"January 23rd, 1868."

This apology was accepted by the writers of the letters that brought it forth; but for all that it was a pity that more independent research was not made by the writer of the *Belgravian* article before compiling it. The article is undeniably incorrect in several particulars besides the obnoxious and scandalous paragraphs, but in authorship as in other walks of life—" *Chacun à son gout.*" The refutation here advanced must be taken as an answer to Captain Gronow's libellous statement, which, in the very first instance is false, as it announces " Mr. Coates' arrival at Bath in 1808 as a person about the age of fifty," whereas when Mr. Coates died in 1848—forty years after—he was only in his seventy-fifth year. From closer inspection of this statement we very much doubt whether the Captain ever saw the performance he describes, more particularly so as an allusion he makes is *almost identical* with one made by the dramatic critic of the *Examiner* for January 31st, 1813, on a representation of Rowe's *Fair Penitent*, in which Mr. Coates sustained the character of Lothario. But enough has been presented to the reader to prove the utter want of truth in the statement put forth by Captain Gronow, and reiterated, we confess without malice, by the late Mr. Walter Thornbury.

Mrs. Boyd survived her first husband for many years—in fact, until the year 1872, when she died at the Oatlands Park Hotel, on Sunday the 15th of September, much lamented by her second husband, Mark Boyd, Esq., as well as by a large and influential circle of friends, many of whom well remembered her as the handsome wife of the then " Well-known Amateur of Fashion." Mrs. Boyd was interred in the vault of her first husband at Kensal Green Cemetery ; which, strange to say, is almost side by side with the family vault of her second husband, in which he has since been placed.

In bringing this biographical sketch to a close, we wish to point out that throughout the whole career of Mr. Coates, and particularly at the eventful epoch of the Regency, we find him pursuing his pleasures as a gentleman, unsullied by any of the vicious habits of that time. In all the depreciatory articles and criticisms upon him that have been published (if we except the libellous one before recorded) none even hinted at any of the then fashionable " vices," which are too well known to need enumeration. These few simple facts alone should convey a tribute to the memory of the late Mr. Robert Coates, as few indeed would have passed through the trying ordeal as an "Amateur of Fashion" without revealing a little of the "seamy side of nature." We might, perhaps, be called to account for overlooking his extravagance; but, again, this was not unwarrantable, before the period of the West Indian troubles. For his losses then he was not to blame; even from this difficulty he ultimately emerged better off than many others, being able to live to a ripe old age, in fairly good style; so that any monetary indiscretions he may have committed in earlier days did not materially deprive him of ample comfort in after life, even conjointly with the depreciation of his West Indian property.

Many have tried to tread the path trodden by Mr. Coates as an "Amateur of Thespis and of Fashion," but all have signally failed. We believe that "Diamond" and "Romeo" Coates will remain uneclipsed as "the greatest dramatic Amateur of the 19th century."

INDEX.

www.ingramcontent.com/pod-product-compliance
Lightning Source LLC
Chambersburg PA
CBHW020353030726
47496CB00007B/2118